Foreword

Gateshead Central Library has a thriving Poetry Reading Group which has been meeting on the third Monday of each month for over 10 years. Some members of the reading group were writing poetry of their own, therefore, in 2012 we decided to start a poetry and prose writing group called Scribblers. The group started very slowly with only two persons attending the first meeting but has grown steadily into a group of twelve regulars.

Over the last eight years Scribblers have worked on a fantastic range of projects, including writing and acting in a Christmas pantomime and presenting a spoken word performance inspired by artwork in the Shipley Gallery. The group offers amateur writers the opportunity to express their creativity in a supportive atmosphere with like-minded people.

Scribblers meet on alternate Fridays at Gateshead Central Library between the hours of 9.30-11.30am and offer a warm and friendly welcome to anyone who comes along.

Gateshead Libraries are proud to support Scribblers and wish the group every success with this publication.

Chris Myhill: Area Manager. Gateshead Library, Prince Consort Road. NE8 4LN

How 'Scribblers' Came To Be

I came to Gateshead library not really knowing if there was
any kind of writing group going

I was told there was not but one starting soon, and they would
ring me back the following afternoon

With great anticipation I came down on the day but there was
only the three of us to my dismay!

Then as word got out and time moved on more people
suddenly started to come along

We were an established writing group at last and chairs around
the table were filling fast!

Pete Ross came later on the scene who filled us with great
ideas and dreams

He asked would we write a performance to show one and all.
Yes, we all said and writing it we had a ball

Our little group now needed to have a name; suggestions were
given until the 'Scribblers' we became

That first play was the start of more to come like writing for
the art gallery which is now an annual one!

Then a pantomime committee which involved just a few was
set up by Pete giving us a different write to do

After months of meetings and sweating over the plots finally it
was ready, so we give it a shot

The children all loved it a great Christmas treat!

Our Harry got a part and so did Pete

There have been many writing opportunities since that time

Like helping local artists with their work who have used our
stories and rhymes

So, looking back on what I have helped to achieve

Scribblers means a great deal to us and me!

Founder Member: Tracey Monaghan

CONTENTS

The Scribblers who have contributed to this collection are listed below.

4

5

The Christmas Angel

Goodness, what was that? Marian stopped and peered around the door into the lounge to see what was causing the commotion. The warden, Christine, and, Matt, the handyman were standing next to a large box in the middle of the floor.

With her hands on her hips Christine stared down into the box. "Oh, no, what a blooming mess!"

Matt chuckled. "Well, we can't put these up this year they're nearly as decrepit as I am."

He scratched his goatee-beard and pulled the bottom of a silver Christmas tree out of the box. Most of the branches were torn and it had turned a motley grey colour. He held it up high. "Yuk, this has seen better days?"

Christine reached down and pulled out a plastic bag full of broken baubles with snapped pieces of tinsel. "What a shame because they were quite pretty."

Matt shook his head and frowned just as Marian walked into the lounge. "Are you having problems?"

Christine looked up and smiled. "Hello, Marian, are you off out for a stroll?"

"Shopping actually," she said. "I was just passing the door when I heard you both."

"Would you just look at this lot, Marian," she moaned in her soft Irish lilt. "I was going to put some Christmas decorations up, but I'll have to think again now."

Marian peered into the box. "Oh, dear, if only they'd been wrapped up properly, they'd still be all right?"

Bending forward Marian rescued the top of the tree from the box. Hanging limply from it was a faded angel with a torn dress and a collection of dirty fuzz where the once golden hair had been. One of her wings was snapped in half and hung precariously as Matt took it from her.

He tossed it back into the box. "The warden we had before Christine couldn't have given a jot about anything. As you can see from this lot, it's a right mess."

"Hmmm," Christine sighed.

Marian wasn't surprised when Christine didn't react. She was too kind-hearted to be mean about other people. She had a genuine smile, that from the day Marian had moved in, filled her with confidence. "It's what I call a leap of faith entering sheltered housing," she'd told Marion. "And, it's important to me that you feel safe."

Christine sank down into a chair. "Maybe we could salvage some of them and try to cover the tree with some new tinsel?"

"Well," Matt mused. "I'll give it a go but don't expect miracles."

Christine brightened. "See what you can do, Matt, and I'll ask on Monday if I can have some money for new ones."

Marian sat down in the chair next to her while Matt picked up the box and plodded out with it.

"So, how are you settling in, Marian?" she asked. "It must be nearly three months now, but we don't see much of you here in the communal lounge with the other residents?"

She tried not to sound ungrateful. "I know, Christine, but I'm not much of a TV fan and I don't play cards," she said. "To be honest, I'm more than happy to sit and read a good book."

Christine smiled and nodded. "Well, that's more than understandable because that's what you're used to doing," she said. "It was bound to be a big change leaving your old house and down-sizing to a self-contained flat?"

A piece of silver tinsel was left behind sticking up out of the carpet. Bending forward Marian picked it up and twirled it between her fingers. "You know, I've had our Christmas decorations at home for nearly forty years and they were all wrapped with the same tissue paper every year then put away as carefully as the first year we bought them."

"Forty years," Christine mused, "that is a long time."

Marian smiled. "Yes, I remember the day my husband, Frank brought the tree and decorations home as if it was yesterday," she said feeling warm inside at the memories. "We'd saved hard to buy them. Our daughter, Jenny, was having her first birthday party on the 21st of December and I'd wanted to put the decorations up for her."

Christine clapped her hands together. "Oh, keep going, Marian, I love Christmas stories."

"Are you sure you've time for this, Christine?"

Christine settled back in the chair. "All the time in the world."

Marian couldn't help but smile thinking of her husband. "Well, I'd given Frank money to buy the tree, six hand painted baubles, and a big angel. He'd arrived home with them all in boxes and had carefully fitted the tree together. I'd slowly peeled back the wrapping from each bauble gasping with delight at each glittery Christmas scene," she said and paused feeling tears prick her eyes. "Then, carefully, we'd hung them one by one with the metal clasp around each branch. Frank brought the stool and I'd placed the angel on the top. She was beautiful in a long white dress with a thin strip of red velvet crossing the bodice and gold wings. We'd both sat back in awe looking at the tree."

Excitedly, Christine said, "I do love an angel at the top of the tree. It's so much better than having a star, and I bet Jenny loved it too?"

Marian grinned. "Well, of course Jenny had been too young to appreciate it that first year, but we'd set our traditions in place for all the Christmas's to come. Frank played Santa Claus every year, creeping between the two rooms with the filled stockings after midnight," she said and swallowed hard. "Jenny always left sherry and mince pies out for Santa, and you know, Christine, they tasted better than any champagne and caviar ever could."

Gently, Christine took her hand. "Take your time, Marian."

She nodded. "Then every year I bought a new bauble to add to the collection. Some did break over the years of course, but the angel had remained as steadfast as the first year we bought her."

Looking up at Christine now, she realised her face was wet with tears. She pulled a tissue from her sleeve and wiped them away. "Even after Frank died and Jenny was grown-up with her own family, I still put the tree up on the 21st December every year. It'll be the first year they've not been out of the boxes since 1960."

"Oh, Marian," she said kindly. "This must be so hard for you. Did you bring the decorations with you?"

She shook her head and gave her a wobbly smile. "I think Jenny took them to her house to store in the attic because there's no room in the flat."

"Okay," Christine murmured. "And is she coming to see you this weekend?"

"Oh yes," she said perking up. "She'll be here with the children at four o'clock. That's why I'm off to the bakery now to buy cake for tea."

"Great, you know, Marian, I'm always here, if ever you want to talk?"

She smiled her thanks, and they got up together heading towards the door.

***

Back in her flat she prepared tea and thought about Christine's kindness, and determined to make more of an effort to make friends with the other residents.

Slicing the Victoria sponge she frowned remembering the first time Jenny came to visit after she'd moved in. Jenny had scanned the lounge to look for her and saw other residents together playing cards. There was music playing and a couple were trying out a new dance.

"But, Jenny, I was in the middle of a good book," she'd said in her flat. However, she'd seen her daughter's lovely face creased with worry.

Marian cringed now knowing Jenny had enough to cope with looking after the children and her work without unnecessary concern about her. She brightened deciding upon a plan.

Ten minutes before Jenny was due, she made her way to the gardens. The sun was lovely, and she held her face up feeling the warmth on her cheeks. She was determined to let Jenny see how settled she was and, how making the move had been the right decision.

Wrapped in her warm coat she settled herself in one of the sun chairs and let her mind drift back to September when she'd had a small black-out and had fallen in the old kitchen. She had no lasting injuries but couldn't remember how or what happened? Hospital tests had proved negative, but her GP had said, "Well, I can't guarantee that you won't have another black-out, so, I'd recommend you move from this old house into a warden-controlled flat, Marian."

Jenny had paled with anxiety at his words. And, although it hadn't been an easy decision, more than anything she'd wanted to give her daughter peace of mind.

Jenny's voice called out now. "Hey, Mum, here you are. I thought you'd be in your flat?"

She got up and grinned at the sight of her daughter bouncing towards her. "I'm just taking in the last of the sunshine, darling."

Marian linked her arm through Jenny's as they walked along to the flat. "I've got tea all ready, but where are the children?"

"Oh, they've gone to a Christmas party," she said as they headed into the kitchen. "Jim's just parking the car."

Dressed in a blue polo neck jumper and jeans Jenny looked no different to when she was a teenager. She hiked herself up onto the bench and sat swinging her legs eating a piece of cake.

Marian switched on the kettle and told her about the commotion in the lounge earlier. "So, I told Christine all about our Christmas decorations," she said. "Is the box still in your attic, Jenny?"

"Yes, Mum, shall we bring it over to put the tree up?"

Marian was just about to answer when Jim sauntered into the kitchen.

"Hi, Mother," he said and kissed her on the cheek. She cringed. Jim always called her that and she hated it.

"Have you told her yet?"

"Jim!" Jenny hissed.

"Told me what, love?"

Marian bit the inside of her cheek. She could feel the atmosphere change and saw Jenny pick at the seam on her jeans.

"Well, Mum," she hedged. "Jim has bought the four of us tickets to go to New York for Christmas."

Marian's earlier brightness seemed to crash to the pit of her stomach knowing she was going to be alone at Christmas.

Jenny stammered, "I, m…mean, it's something Jim, well, me and the children have wanted to do for ages. And, because you are being so well looked after here, we thought…" her voice faded, and her face flushed pink.

Marian could see the distress in her daughters' eyes. She knew instantly it hadn't been her idea to go to New York but the tactless clown that she was married to.

She looked at his patronising expression as he jutted out his pointy chin hoping to cause upset between them. But she forced a bright smile onto her face. "Jenny, what a marvellous treat!"

"Oh, Mum, the kids are so excited," she said. "You will be okay here though, won't you?"

"Of course, I will," she retorted. "Whatever makes you think I wouldn't?"

Jenny's face brightened and she raised her eyebrow. "You sure, Mum?"

She cocked her head and smirked at her son-in-law to let him know he'd never come between her and Jenny then tutted. "I'll be just fine, now stop talking nonsense and tell me all about the trip."

***

After waving goodbye in the car park Marian turned slowly and made her way back into the hall. The thought of spending Christmas alone in the flat made her throat tense and she took a deep breath. As she passed the lounge a male voice called out which startled her.

"She's a lovely lass, I bet you're proud of her?" he said.

She saw a small frail man sitting in one of the chairs smiling at her and crossed over to him.

"Do you mean, my Jenny?"

He nodded. "Aye, she's really friendly. She always has a word with me as she passes by. Although, I can't say the same for the tall chap that's usually with her?"

"Oh, that's my wonderful son-in-law," she snorted and rolled her eyes.

Marian saw his blue eyes twinkle and he burst out laughing. "He's that good, eh?"

She sat down in the chair next to him. "Well, he definitely wouldn't have been my choice for her," she said. "Because I think she deserves much better. But he was her choice, so, I have to grin and bear it."

"You're lucky to have her," he sighed. "I don't have any family left now. I never married and lived all my life with my twin brother, Mike who died last year."

She gasped and felt her cheeks flush thinking how dreadful her life would have been without Frank and Jenny.

A small thermos flask was on the table next to him. "Fancy a cuppa?"

"That'd be lovely, thanks," she said smiling.

Marian watched his dainty hands pour tea into a cup then reach down into the other side of the chair and pull out a packet of custard cream biscuits.

He offered her the packet. "Go, on, you look as though you could do with something sweet?"

She nodded and munched on a biscuit while drinking the hot tea. Her spirits lifted. "By the way, I'm Marian," she said. "Will you be here at Christmas? Sorry, I don't know your name?"

He grinned. "It's Tom, and yes, I'll be here," he said. "It's my home now. We had to sell the old house when Mike died."

"Me, too, it's not easy is it?" she said sighing. "It feels very strange moving to a new place after fifty years."

"You're not kidding, but there again, we didn't celebrate Christmas much in the house. We never saw the point of decorations and the most we ever did was treat ourselves to a decent turkey. Mike was a great cook; I'll say that for him."

Quietly, she said, "I've been feeling sorry for myself because I won't be at Jenny's having my usual Christmas. And, I'd forgotten there are some people who have never been as fortunate as me."

"Well, Marian, you know the old saying. What you've never had, you never miss…"

They both lapsed into silence and Marian could tell Tom was as lost in his memories as she was.

He brightened. "Although we should have a good time here together because Christine and Matt are doing their best to dress the place up a bit," he said. "And we're going to have a special Christmas lunch all together in the dining room."

She smiled. "Oh, that'll be nice, Tom."

She stayed in the lounge until nine o'clock that night watching TV with Tom and some of the other residents.

Two ladies had brought old board games with them and they'd all laughed reciting memories of their families playing Monopoly and cheating at Snakes & Ladders. Marian listened to stories about New Year's Eve parties and Christmas Day antics, and could tell their memories were just as precious as hers.

***

The next morning, Marian felt more upbeat and determined to make the best of whatever Christmas would bring. At the sound of the intercom buzzer to her flat, she hurried along the hall to see Jenny carrying a large box through the door.

Marian gasped with delight. It was their Christmas box. She ran her hand lovingly along the side of the box. "Oh, Jenny," she murmured.

"I thought I'd bring them over and even if we can't get them all up in the flat, we can at least put the tree up for you."

When they turned to walk along the corridor, Matt appeared in the lounge doorway with a hammer in his hand. "Blooming Christmas tree," he grumbled. "It's well and truly finished. As soon as I've got the branches sorted out the base has collapsed!"

Marian thought quickly. "Thanks, Jenny," she said. "But I'd like to put the decorations and tree in the lounge so that everyone can enjoy them."

Christine appeared and peered around Matt. "Oh, Marian, thank you, what a wonderful gesture."

"Right then," Jenny said brightly. "Let's get started."

Matt carried the box to the middle of the lounge and started to lift everything out. Christine and Jenny decided the table in the bay window would be the best place for the tree.

Tom, who was sitting in his usual place got up. "Aye now, what's all this?"

Matt moved his chair closer and Marian explained what Jenny had done. "So, Tom, we'll have the decorations to look at all over the holidays."

Matt and Jenny started fitting the tree together. Christine put a CD on with a choir singing Christmas carols and when the other residents heard the music, they all drifted inside the lounge.

Everyone's spirits rose while they sang along, and Jenny started to dress the tree. Marian unwrapped each bauble to exclamations of Ooh's and Aah's at the glittery Christmas scenes. Matt checked the fairy lights and entwined them through the branches then Jenny handed the last box to her. She lovingly peeled the cotton wool away to reveal the angel. She was as beautiful as ever. Marian walked up to the tree and smiling proudly she placed her on the top.

Christine switched the lights on with a whooping, "Merry Christmas Everyone!"

Marian turned from the tree to see Tom's eyes misted with tears and beamed at him.

"Now there's a sight for sore eyes," he murmured.

A warm glow of happiness filled her, and she smiled. "I think we're going to have a lovely Christmas after all."

Susan Willis

A Night At The Library

Bronwen Lewis a fifty-eight-year-old greying haired spinster plainly dressed in knee length woollen plaid skirt and worn red jumper with flat black pointed shoes toiled over her beloved books in the library of the small welsh town of Risca. She had a passion for books and could not get enough of the stories they revealed, reading them from beginning to end in one sitting. Being very protective over her books she seemed the ideal employee for the small-town library. But she never wanted anyone to actually borrow the books, they didn't take care of them like she did, often proven when books returned with tea stains, crayon drawings and even crossings out in red pen! She would feel infuriated at the borrower for defiling her books, but her complaints were pushed aside by her manager saying as long as no pages were missing, she should put them back onto the shelves. This left Bronwen feeling powerless.

As she got closer to retirement age Bronwen grew crankier about the treatment of her books, made no polite conversation, just peered over her glasses at people and scoured, earning her a nickname of 'Old Sour Face'. When anyone came to her desk with their books, she would hammer the stamp down so hard it made them jump, much to her amusement. Then one fateful night after closing time perched on a high ladder, she lost her balance and fell, the library deserted no one heard her cries, she lay all night on the floor with just her books for comfort. The following morning cleaners came in and found Bronwen dead. Her funeral was presided over by her chapel minister, she had no family and no real friends, and was buried with no mourners, in the local cemetery. The town actually celebrated her demise, and eagerly awaited the new recruit to the library the following week. But it was not going to be that easy!

Ann Jones a thirty something year old dressed in the latest fashion of mini skirt, blouse and high heels adorned with blond flowing locks saw the notice in the window advertising for a librarian in her local town and applied for the position. Following a successful interview, she agreed to work the evening before the opening to ensure everything was in its place, leaving her free to greet the townspeople the following day. She went along to the library on the Sunday evening, it was eerie in the dark, and the lights were dim. Walking along the shelves suddenly the air turned cold, the hairs stood up on the back of her neck. She heard a groaning noise and turned only to find a ghostly figure peering at her over glasses with menacing eyes, "Get out of my library girl, you don't belong here, these are my precious books," she screeched at her.

Ann was so frightened she ran and hid around the corner out of view, or so she thought, "I said get out of my library."

Ann needing no more persuasion fled through the great doors.

No one has ever been found to replace Bronwen yet, for some reason applicants are keen, but never seem to turn up on the Monday morning!

Tracey Monaghan

The Uniform He Wore

It was the uniform he wore
It was the closing of a door
It was his father saying
"Son, you've made me proud"
It was his mother's hopes and fears
It was her fighting back the tears
It was the closing of a door
It was the uniform he wore.

It was 'goodbye' to 'little Bill'
It was 'hello' to march and drill
It was 'grow up. And do it fast'
It was "how long will this thing last?"
It was the closing of a door
It was the uniform he wore.

It was the uniform he'd worn
Shredded, stained and torn
It was the closing of *his* door
'Damn the uniform he wore'

Maureen C Bell

And Then

A ray of sun shone strongly through the many holes and gaps of my home. For my home was a kind of a large kennel, but really, just a shack. This is where I was born about eight weeks ago. My lovely loving mother often licked me all over, as I lay on a bed of straw and a large blanket. Her milk was delicious, her teats had swelled, and my mouth encompassed them. My brother and sister also shared the six teats.

Every morning my mother's keeper would place a bowl of meat and biscuit for her to devour. Opening our door about six in the morning to give her a feed, and at about six in the evening she gave her a large bowl of water and, some more meat.
But one April day my mother's keeper reached into our kennel with two long arms and picked both my sister and me into her arms. Little did I know but this was the day I would depart from my loving family. Walking through the farmyard, me and my sister, the constant sound of ewes bleating, and the cry of the lambs will remain in my mind forever.

And then, as we reach the big steel gates of my farm, two human strangers appeared. Two figures, two other humans. The sounds and muffles I could not comprehend filled my ears. Human chatter and handshakes. Eventually my keeper handed me over to the strangers. Mother came rushing over, she seemed happy to see them. They gave her tit bits of some kind of food and she greedily devoured them. And then! At that moment my departure from my loving mother began.

The strange new world outside my gated home was big. Huge fields of sheep and cattle and horses and my lovely home, were about to disappear forever.

Holding me in their arms, I began to panic. Where was I going? I want me mother. But firmly they clasped me as they walked to a certain box with wheels.

My lovely little world was gone, and I would plummet into this strange new world of sounds and places and obstacles.

Reflection:
I'm thinking of what my pup could be thinking.

Tom Gallagher

Beverage

A cuppa tea this morning, Yorkshire, Earl Grey or Tips,
To wake my mind from slumber, I slowly take small sips,
A coffee at elevenses, refresh, revive, reform,
A creamy cup of a roasted bean to bring me back to norm,
A mug of soup at lunch time, tomato, veg or oxtail,
A nice hot drink for me to sink, my vigour to prevail,
A nice cold pint this evening, to get me in the mood,
A slurp or two, a drink with you, before we have our food,
Hot chocolate for my bedtime, I'll hold you in my arms,
A nice cool cup for me to supp, before I give my charms,

Tom Gallagher

The First Day of Autumn

It's raining today not with rain but with leaves,
As I wait for a bus, they fall down from the trees.
Autumn I thought in my head.
As they swirled in a lane golden and red,
A breeze floats them down to the ground.
And whirls and twirls them around and around,
The day is dull and dark clouds are grey.
Today blue skies have gone away.
Swirling and twirling they pass me by.
Creating a patterned carpet as they lie.
Mother nature has turned out her light.
Grey days no longer bright.
A carpet of colour lies in place.
As one by one they fall and chase.
A magical sight for us to see.
As the next fall of leaves fall down from the trees.
Yes, the first day of autumn in my mind's eye.
As another gush of leaves go rushing by.

Mandy Baharie

Eloping

A single ray of light pierced the forest canopy, faintly illuminating the spot for her tryst with Peter. Her heart was pounding in her breast. If they were caught, Peter would probably be tortured and executed, and she would be forced to marry that ugly giant of a man. Urrgh, she shivered at the thought.

There was no sign of Peter. She wondered, had he been able to get away unseen? The castle was alive with guests, and retainers were hurrying back and forth, preparing for the evenings feast and the morning nuptials.

She slowly approached that spot, pushing herself through the thickets, slowly, quietly, to make as little noise as possible. They should not be accidentally discovered this close to the castle.

Her maid was to meet them early next day, five miles away at The Fighting Cocks. She would bring her pack and Peter was to acquire horses for their escape. That itself was a hanging matter.

The maid had given her father the excuse that she was indisposed and could not attend the feast to celebrate her wedding the following day. A wedding, she thought sadly, already her belly was giving her that sickly feeling and she would frequently throw up. Yes, she certainly was indisposed.

'Mary, is that you?' She heard him whisper as he rose out of the bracken at the centre of that spot of light. She hurried to him and he enfolded her in his arms. She clung to him not wanting him to let her free, but they must make haste. They must reach The Fighting Cocks before dawn, when her absence would be noted, and all hell would break loose.

'I would go to hell with you,' she told him.

He smiled, 'We may yet end up there if we do not hurry.'

Once clear of the forest, they set forth at a brisk walk across fields and meadows keeping clear of the main tracks to avoid unwanted attention. They skirted a few small villages and hamlets, all part of her father's domain in case anyone should happen to recognise her. She was a popular visitor to her father's estates and often distributed alms on her visits there.

The moon had got well past its zenith and was starting to wane, and the sky was clear as they approached The Fighting Cocks. They halted in a small copse of trees a short way from the inn. Soon it would be dawn.

Peter said, 'Wait here because we don't want anyone to recognise you.'

He went forward and disappeared from her view. She pulled her shawl tightly around her head and shoulders. She was starting to feel the cold but knew that later when the sun rose it would be a glorious hot day, and she would have to shield her face to avoid recognition. His absence seemed interminable and she shivered slightly hidden away in the shade.

Her heart skipped a beat, there he was leading two horses. He raised his hand to halt her as she started to walk towards him. Quietly, he approached her then they reunited into the heart of the copse where he started to dig into a pile of bracken, exposing two packs. He opened one and pulled out some rags.

'Quickly, change into these,' he said. 'You will not be as easily recognised in them.'

Walking the horses, they returned about a mile to where, in another stand of trees they met Mary's maid, Sarah. She had brought her mistresses possessions in another pack. Then, being enough distance from The Fighting Cocks they mounted the horses, called goodbye to Sarah, and as the first rays of the morning sun rose above the horizon they set off at a tangent heading to the north and hopefully, happiness together.

Mary had left a note for her father, advising him of her regret at running away to her uncle in Devon. She was sorry but she did not yet feel ready for marriage.

They'd thought this might give them a good start if her father chased after her to Devon, they could get well on their way North and loose themselves among the moors and towns of Cumberland and Yorkshire. They hoped a village friar would perhaps marry them, bearing in mind her condition. A monk somewhere they were convinced would welcome a little piece of silver, no questions asked.

The further north they progressed. The more relaxed they became but never stopping more than two or three days anywhere. Mary knew her father. She knew he would never give up seeking her, to the ends of the earth. They kept clear of the main thoroughfares of the villages and country, and just kept to the lesser used tracks and paths near habitation. Mary was sure her father would have discovered her deception and the hunt would have started.

The small amount of coin they had mustered for their escape plan was slowly diminishing as they progressed north, and Peter had started seeking casual work to eke out their reserve. Two days here to help repair field boundaries and a day there to drive cattle to market. This was slowing down their progress, but a bigger shock awaited them as they approached a crossroad. There, nailed to the signpost, they discovered a notice. Peter was unable to read, but the message was clear, they had a price on their heads.

Where could they hide? Where could they go? The whole countryside would be on the lookout for them now. Who would not turn his own granny in for a hundred pounds especially in this, to them, foreign region?

They decided to go off the worn tracks and headed away from civilisation making their way over the rough ground towards the moors. Mary was finding it hard going, her swollen belly was getting more and more uncomfortable. Every step of her horse was sending uncomfortable feelings through her whole being. But with Peter's love and support, she knew she had to bear it.

Peter was searching the rocks around them for the easiest route up the hillside for Mary's sake. Out of the corner of his eye he saw movement behind them. They were found. What should they do?

'I just can't go back there to that monster,' Mary pleaded.

'Keep climbing,' Peter told her. 'As fast as you can.'

Up and up they went but were eventually halted at the edge of a great chasm.

They were trapped. They turned to face their hunters waiting patiently and expressing their undying love for each other. Her father approached her, but she clung tightly to her lover.

'I'm sorry father,' she said holding Peter tightly.

Her father was taken aback at the sight of her enormous belly.

'You, young fool,' he chastised her.

He advanced to strike Peter with this sword. Mary clung to her lover and pushed hard against the rocky cliff edge.

'I love you,' she whispered softly to him as they fell.

***

It was a three-mile trek along the cliff edge and down the first pass into the chasm. Lord Shrewsbury was eager to recover the body of his youngest daughter. She was a mirror image of his beloved wife who had lost her life bringing Mary into the world.

Full of remorse and regret from the loss of his daughter and her unborn son, his only grandson, he had his retainers recover both broken bodies. Forgiving his daughter and her lover, he had them interred together in a tomb within Shrewsbury Cathedral, where they have rested together now for over five hundred years.

Harry Mason

Housewife's Plea
Free me from this domestic life
give me to time to think
Free me from all my chores
unchain me from the sink
Free me from cooking and washing
loosen these ropes that bind
Free me from cleaning and dusting
let me clear my mind
Free me from troubles and strife
See me as your wife

Who Am I?
I am the endless sea with hidden depths
I am the cliffs reaching up towards the sky
I am the full moon beaming for all to see
I am the stars at night blinking in the dark
I am the soft rains falling silently down
I am the sun rays warming up the earth
I am the light breezes rustling through the trees
I am thunder breaking through the silence
I am lightning startling, thrilling all below
I am mother earth with more secrets yet untold

Tracey Monaghan

Winter

These long weeks with winters chill
I'm dreading next month's big gas bill
That sun-drenched coast seen on TV
We need it here, so let it be

It's just not fair, they get all the sun
This cold wet Isle is just no fun
The daffodils have flowered too late
Those golden blooms, we'll have to wait

The farmers' fields are soaking wet
On Grand National day, I'll have a bet
Let's hope the going is good and sound
As usual, I'll lose my pound

The weatherman says sun next week
These last few weeks have been so dreek
The birds are singing this early morn
Think sunny days and fields of corn

Tom Gallagher

Spellbound.

For the first time in many years, I passed the shop in Seymour Street. I had been walking, no, wandering around in a fruitless pursuit of diversion. On the lookout for anything which would wrench my attention from the lurid visions, scalding my mind. I stopped, I don't remember physically stopping, it must have been automatic, a kernel of memory boiling up from the sub-conscious. Something was different, in 1913, this had been a German bookshop with a German name, Schmidt's books that was it, the name now read Smith's Book's. I found myself entering this place in somewhat morbid anticipation of what the war had done to its owners. Was I hoping to see pain and suffering in their eyes, if indeed, they were still there? After all this was the race that had butchered my men, half blinded, and scarred me for life, leading to what they euphemistically term 'shell shock'.

On entering everything appeared as it was, the neat shelves stacked with books, the paying desk with its antique cash machine, even the smell was the same, gently ageing print, - a hint of tobacco smoke. Herr Schmidt smiled benevolently at me as I pretended to examine a book on the ' Pride and Power of the British Empire.' I felt physically sick, then began shaking from head to foot.

"Are you alright sir? Papa will fetch you a drink of water. Sit here please," she said.

Through the tears streaming down my face I could see it was Maria, Schmidt's daughter, she had been but a child the last time I saw her, -just a wisp of a girl. Now she was full grown to womanhood.

"It's just that," I mumbled.

"I know!" She whispered, " I have nursed hundreds of boys through this, here take my hand."

I took her hand, it was soft, healing, electric, with her other hand she massaged my ruptured face, whilst all the time murmuring, "It will be alright, it will be alright, it will be alright!"

Her love and devotion wrought in me such a rapid epiphany, that at last, a besieged, and wounded mind conceded that perhaps, just perhaps, she might be right.

Barry Ross

How I Miss Jadatti's Kiss

My beautiful Jadatti, white hair poking from her hijab, cooking mamounia for us all. Mama and Papa were still with us then, the whole family together. Her face was wise, wrinkles hewn by watching her country at war. She would hug me close and tell me that all would be well. She'd fill up my beautiful blue bowl. And I could believe that all would be well.

Using the sliver of light, I can see the darkened outline of the door. The watery shaft of whiteness squeezing beneath gives maybe five percent illumination. Edie would be proud of me working out five percent. I hated percentages. And the word illumination. 'It's a top notch one,' she'd say.

But five percent is enough. Squeezing my eyelids almost together, the rectangular shape of the window is just visible. Curtains, big and heavy, nailed across it. Red, blood red, curtains with tassels around the edge, and a pattern. The tassels are starting to come apart, some threads hang lower than others. The smell that lingers in the fabric, that aroma of fried kubbeh and kabsah, it was our happy food. It transports me back to my shack in camp, to the white tarpaulin ceilings with red Safe For Children logos flapping up in the hot, dusty wind. When the direction changed, deflated by the gusts, the tarpaulins would press down on us. It sounded so scary that sudden crack, and the flicking movement would make us all laugh out loud. Moments of those long days when I could forget I was alone.

I ache for the wind to press down on me now.

Echoing voices outside my room cause my stomach to heave. Quiet talk in low voices. They laugh sometimes, spit and cuss, complain the price is too high.

I cannot recall how my laugh sounds, how to make that noise. It has been silenced by the unwelcome learning.

The scraping of dirty stubble against my cheek leaves my skin hot and red and raw.

What a man weighs, heavy against my body, squeezing out the life I have left. The smell of them - hair tainted with cigarette smoke, with grease, with engine oil.

Kisses forged through moustached mouths, blackened teeth, tobacco-tasting tongues. The grunting heave as they squirm. Low voices full of syllables and sounds from worlds unknown to me.

They never say my name.

Their noises remind me of those nights in camp. Different languages swirling around in the wind, odd words making sense. Amena used to remind me of how I'd arrived at camp. My feet bled on the walk. Dust created red crusts inside my sandals. A sharpened pencil still clutched in my hand. She told me how her family would want her to get to Europe, finish her education.

'It is all I can do to make them proud now they are gone,' she'd say. Together with Edie, she was my new family. They must've overheard her chatter about going to school in England.

'We can fast track you,' they'd promised. 'Our friends will sort your papers and places in good schools, find your families. Come.'

Edie's words haunt me still. Warning we should only trust the aid workers. We'd giggled when we first met her. Our new carer, she said. She made us sound precious with that word, safeguarding.

Alone on this filthy bed I wonder did Edie look for us, report us missing next day when we didn't turn up for her kabsah? When our shack was silent and empty?

When the bowl arrives at the end of each day, the door opens just enough to place the food on the floor. The five percent light is turned back on. Then, the click of the lock. I sweep my hand over the cool tiled floor to locate the bowl. It's never the kubbeh they cook for themselves.

As I eat, the darkness is my friend. Today's semolina as tasteless as yesterday's, encrusts the rim but still takes me back to Jadatti's mamounia.

Served in my blue glazed bowl, topped with cinnamon and pistachio nuts. Its sweetness lingering in my mouth then followed by a kiss, a rain of kisses, as she'd tell me that I would become our country's next president, or maybe a pilot or an architect.

Alwyn Bathan

Knitting

CAN WE WORK THE PATTERN OUT?

Wool gathering one day

I saw you, and it seems

You've wound yourself around me,
You're part of all my dreams

My heart's on pins and needles
My nerves are knitted tight
My tensions all to Hell,
You have to put things right.

Don't cast me off,
Don't stitch me up
Until you know my mind
Don't move me
onto a spare pin,
I'm not the waiting kind.

Be plain my lovely girl,
my purl.
Whisper softly whether,
if we work the pattern out,
we can be
2 tog
forever.

LET ME BE YOUR COMFORTER
Take the endless
thread of my love,
Cast on – begin
Shape me
Knit me
inextricably,
Into the pattern of your life.
Wind me around you
Let me protect you
against the frosty winds

THE KNITTING'S OVER
Pin me out on the table
of your dreams.
Press me with the steaming iron
of your passion.
I'm loopy about you.

Maureen C Bell

My War: The Devil Inside

21 August 1917

Dear Mam,

You remember John. He was my best friend. You made him his tea. You said he was a nice lad. All through school we stuck together. Apprentices together. So lucky to be taken on at Matthews, they were cutting down on Apprenticeships because of the war, but we were lucky, always lucky we were, me and John.

You said he was a nice lad. Two peas in a pod you said. You were pleased we were called up together. We joined the DLI. Just 18 years old in 1917, both of us born within two months of each other. You knew we would watch out for each other. You said he was a nice lad Mam and you were right. You said we would be okay as long as we stuck together.

After initial training camp we set out for France in an old Ferry. We crossed the Channel, half an hour and landed in Calais. There were thousands of us Mam, but we stuck together, me and John. We were sent to Arras, to attack the Germans. Watching, waiting, marching, keeping safe Mam that's what we did, keeping safe.

John is dead Mam. Did I tell you John is dead? I can still see his face every minute of the day; I can still see his bloody face. It is changing shape Mam, his face. I do not recognise him anymore. He has become a monster now Mam, he is inside of me, he is a monster inside of me. But you said he was a nice lad.

Those Germans knew what they were doing. After the mines went off and we broke through, they just waited and then let us have it as we advanced through their lines Mam. We never saw them until it was too late. We heard the rat tat tat and the shells exploding, and all ran for cover, falling to the ground, rat a tat tat, rat a tat tat Mam.

Then it was quiet. I looked up, I was Ok, so were lots of lads. Time to get up and get at the Hun. I spotted John still lying, so I shouted, "Come on John". He did not move Mam, so I kept on shouting "come on John, we need to get out". I did not want to go over, but I ran to him Mam as fast as I could. He was in a bad way Mam; I only remember his face. His eyes were open, wide open. I held his hand Mam it was still warm. I covered him and waited with him, not talking just waiting. Such a nice lad Mam, two peas in a pod. I had to leave him there, they told me to leave him, they would look after him. I had to leave him Mam.

I do not know how long it is been, days just go by, turn into weeks and months. I keep marching, keeping safe, with the other lads, doing my bit for King and country. John is dead, but he is still with me, he is part of me. He talks to me, but when I see him, I am frightened Mam. He tells me what to do but I cannot look at his face Mam, his bloody face.

We were only 18. You said he was a nice lad. Two peas in a pod you said. We stuck together.

I am OK but missing the family, thanks for the parcel.

I wish this bloody thing would just stop.

Here's another daft letter I have written to you in my diary, which of course you will never receive.

Love

Harry

Maria Barrell

A Poem inspired by programme notes on C.D. of Beethoven's Sixth Symphony,

'The Pastoral.'

Awakening of Cheerful Feelings upon Arrival in the Country:
Iron clad wheels slowly crunch to a halt
The Steady clip clopping of hooves are stilled
We alight into the surrounding green
A myriad of changing shades and hues
Thirst quenched from a cool babbling brook
Dappled sunlight filters forest canopy
Lightening the shade and lifting our mood

Scene by the Brook
We rest a while and revive by the brook
Far away the sound of merrymaking
Cattle are lowing and sheep bleat from the hills
Nearby farmyard sounds fill the air
A barking dog clucking gobbling of fowl
Birds flit from branch to bough
Filling the air with their sweet music

Merry Gathering of Country Folk
The merrymakers by now amongst us
Carry us along with their jolly revelry
We sing we dance swirling twirling
To merry pipe and drum round and around
The merry dance leads us until we are spent
We rest a while, but the dance carries on
Slowly moving away the breeze quickening

Thunderstorm Shepherd's Song
The sky darkens clouds build covering the sun
Far off a flash of light a rolling sound
That culminates in a tremendous crash
Again, and again the flash and the crash
Then it is gone, and the sun reappears
And far off the shepherd sings that all is well

Happy and Thankful Feelings after the Storm
Peace restored the birds return to sweet song
Merrymakers scattered to their homes
Cattle and sheep return to their grazing and
We give thanks that all is back to normal
The brook now in full spate continues on
Making its merry way toward the ocean
And we go back to our homes thankful
That nature has returned to normality

Harry Mason

Time
Time flies
Time is on your side
Time waits for no man
Time on your hands
Time to live
Time to forgive
Time to pray
Time to play
Time to scream
Time to dream
Time for tea
Time to read
Time to sow
Time to know
Time to sing
Time to win
Time to think
Time to drink
Time to laugh
Time for a bath
Time to hate
Time to wait
Time to cry
Time to say goodbye

Tracey Monaghan

Walking Through the Castle
I had a flask and you may ask
What did it have inside?
Whiskey, Gin or Rum or Tea
Each time I'd quaff it made me pee
Hot cups of soup, I'd drink with relish
But drinking booze, my headache's hellish
Those handy vessels, will soothe your tummy
The booze is good, but soup is yummy

They Fell
Like Ninepins, like Skittles,
like corn to be cut at harvest time
Brave young man and corn, cut in their prime

But young men slaughtered
That awful sound of a rat a tat tat, a rat a tat tat!
One of man's awful inventions
Not a scythe, no not a scythe as such
But it does the same job with utter efficiency

Nurtured and raised by a mother's love
Nurtured and raised by a fertile soil
One to be consumed
The other but consumed by grief

Tom Gallagher

Bensham Grove: It Was on My Patch

I walked the streets of Bensham, plying my trade night and day
Everybody knew me; there was little I need say
My profession is said to be the oldest that is known to man
My competence is undisputed, I deliver where I can
The people who lived in Bensham, afforded me some respect
They saw me as a necessity, for those I did affect
I had my fellow workers, but Bensham was my patch
They left me to my labours, bar if illness I did catch
There was a place in Bensham that I gazed on from the street
A house that was so splendid, its occupants I would never meet
My services were not requested, from those gentle folks within
Bensham Grove was my glimpse of heaven, from a life that
could be grim
I passed the Grove so often, as I delivered my busy trade
The house became my solace, my comfort and my aide
It soon became my guiding light, giving me strength to work
the town
The foundation stone of Bensham, the Jewel in its Crown
Unlike the Grove I became weary, the days felt so much longer
Bensham was now changing, to adapt I needed to be stronger
I was but a mere mortal, my time was coming to an end
I was happy working my patch in Bensham, making many a
good friend
And now there is no work for me, the need for my services
have gone
My haven is still there of course, the Grove remains
welcoming and strong
Now women have their babies in hospital, but fond memories I
do treasure
Being a Bensham Community Midwife, remains my greatest
pleasure

Maria Barrell

Eye Candy
While sitting watching by the sea
Someone distracted me!
Wow eye candy number one to the right
Oh my God what a sight.
His toned body lean and tanned
Lying on the golden sand.

Looking around at the view
Oh my God eye candy number two.
His shoulder length hair, with hands running through it
He posed for a bit, he had it he knew it!

After a while glancing at the sea
Oh my God eye candy number three.
Coming out of the water after taking a swim
Glistening in the sun, he had a body on him.

As I watch the rolling tide
I glance at my love by my side.
Thinking I can't take anymore
Oh my God eye candy number four.
His face with a glowing tan,
He beats them all my gorgeous man!

Mandy Baharie

The Elite Bar

Sitting in the elite bar helping ourselves to drinks
I smiled as our glasses clinked.
Relaxed and happy for all the world to see
There's no place right now I'd rather be.
I went to the bar our glasses were empty
There were quality drinks a variety and plenty.
I had a glass of wine, but no glass for the beer.
A fellow saw me looking, he said "There just here"
He handed me the glass, I had the beer and wine.
"Thank you" I said "That will do fine"
He held on to the glass and gave me a smile
We stood for a second, but it seemed a long while.
"Thanks" I said as he started to linger
"I'm sorry" he said "You've trapped my finger"
Looking down at the bottle, wine and glass.
His finger was trapped, we couldn't help but laugh!

Mandy Baharie

Shipley

Tucked around a corner is a treasure to behold
With paintings, crafts and sculptures and a lot more
Once inside its doors your eyes fill with pleasure
As you gaze around the gallery exploring at your leisure
Joseph Shipley bequeathed his art for generations to enjoy
He acquired many paintings and had collectors in his employ
His wish for the people of Gateshead of whom he had in mind
Was to build a new gallery in which to display his precious finds
It was stipulated that entry be free to one and all
So people can drop in as they pass by on a stroll
The younger generation now enjoy the gallery too
Attending craft making with paper, card, feathers and glue
Exhibitions and crafts often featured from all over the world
Can lose you in their mystery as their secrets come unfurled
Local artists display their paintings bringing memories to the fore
As they jolt pictures from the past leaving you wanting more!

Tracey Monaghan

Meet Me at the Eiffel Tower

'Well, Angela, you know the old saying, a holiday will either make you or break you.'

And she knew her friend, Anne, was right. But she didn't want Peter to break away from her. She loved her husband and always had done. She wanted to make them right again.

They were in the hairdressers and as she waited for the new golden-honey colour to dry she drooled over the holiday details. 'The hotel is just across the road from The Eiffel Tower,' she said. 'Paris is where we spent our very first weekend away together when we were only twenty-three and were mad about each other.'

Anne sighed. 'Are things no better? I mean, have you talked to him about it again?'

They'd been growing apart, slowly but surely, since Christmas and she felt increasingly alone. Some days she felt lost in her own sadness.

'I tried a few weeks ago but he just poo poo'd the fact that there is anything wrong,' she said shrugging her shoulders. 'I've asked if everything is okay at work and he says it's fine, but he's travelling more and more for meetings and conferences.'

She bit her lip. 'And, the bedroom? Well, that's just a room we sleep in now. On the odd occasion we are together, the act holds no loving, it just satisfies a need. I miss us, Anne. I miss the way we've always been together.'

Anne brightened. 'Oh, just you wait, Angela,' she said squeezing her hand. 'Paris in Springtime will get you both full of Ooh La La!'

Angela hurried home to pack their cases. With her case opened out on the bed she packed the new pale-pink spotty dress and pink high heels. Excitement churned in her stomach when she decided to wear the special dress on their first night.

Peter was finishing up a conference in Lyon and travelling up to Paris to join her, so she still had to pack his case for the weeks holiday. Folding clean T-shirts into his case she remembered their many holidays in the south of France when their daughter, Kate was a little girl. They'd all loved the French way of life and touring around the campsites.

Kate had popped in yesterday for a cuppa. 'Mum, what's wrong with you and Dad?' she'd asked. 'I haven't heard you mention the swimming pool, your golf, or your long rambling walks lately…' she paused and looked directly at her. 'Well, what I mean, is you and Dad don't seem to spend any time together nowadays?'

Kate was just getting over her divorce and she didn't want her to worry, so she'd put on her cheerful face. 'Oh, we're absolutely fine, love. Your dads just incredibly busy at work.' But Kate had raised her pencilled eyebrow as if to say she didn't believe her. And she couldn't blame her.

***

The flight left on time from Glasgow and Angela laid her head back as the plane soared high-up into the sky. She focussed on her surroundings and practised her deep breathing exercises.

Two years ago, she'd began to suffer from panic attacks which were frightening to someone who'd always enjoyed good mental health. The first time it had happened was in a store changing room when she was trying on jeans. Her heart had begun to race and palpitate, and the walls seemed as if they were closing in on her. She'd thought she was having a heart attack. At the hospital they'd told her all her physical signs were normal and that the episode had probably been a panic attack. Her GP had been amazing. 'Even though you're not due to retire until the age of sixty-six now, if possible, I'd leave the stressful job of teaching and find some quieter past times, Angela.'

She'd relayed the conversation to Peter, who'd agreed. 'Look, darling. Financially we're in a good position. We don't need the money you make, and, I'd rather have you well and at home following the doctor's orders.'

So, she had retired, and it had taken a while, but with medication and cognitive awareness sessions she'd so far, learnt how to manage the attacks, of which she now had very few.

**

From the taxi drivers first, 'Bonjour Madame,' she was enchanted and settled back to enjoy the ride through the city. Looking from one side window to another she breathed in the unique magic of Paris. Her French was good, and she managed a little dialogue with him until they reached the hotel.

The hotel room was perfect with a small balcony looking out to The Eiffel Tower. She flung open the long doors and gasped at the view. She breathed in all of Paris's smells and sounds. A man in a small car and a lorry driver were having a heated dispute about parking at the end of the road and she smiled, the French loved a good argument.

Just as she'd sat down with a gin and tonic from the mini bar, a text arrived. 'Sorry, sweetheart, the train has left Lyon two hours late, so I'll be a while yet. Can you get room service?'

Angela looked over at the pink dress hanging on the wardrobe door and slowly got up to put it inside. You won't be wearing that tonight, she thought sadly, and answered Peter's text with a simple, 'Okay.'

Looking through the menu card she sipped her drink and let her thoughts drift back to their conversation last month about his retirement.

Peter was still working as a CEO for a major company and had the same retirement age of sixty-six. He'd spent the Sunday morning complaining about staying in a basic Travel Lodge in London.

'It won't be long now until you retire,' she'd said cheerfully. 'Then all the trashy travelling will be done with and you'll be able to relax all day at home.'

He'd looked horrified at her suggestion. 'But I can't sit around in the house all day…' he'd said staring at his travel bag. 'Maybe I should try some voluntary work to get me out from under your feet?'

Angela had swallowed a lump in her throat and couldn't find the words to answer him. She'd headed out into the garden to hide the hurt that had engulfed her. Since when was the thought of spending all day with so abhorrent, she'd thought shaking her head in bewilderment. In the past he'd always been glad to be under her feet, or simply just to be with her?

Peter arrived in the hotel room late looking dishevelled after the long six-hour journey on the train. He gave her a quick peck on the cheek. 'The train journey was horrendous it took hours longer than it should have. There was no food or drinks left in the café bar, and because we were late into every station, it's just got further and further behind all the way up the country!'

He wolfed down a Croc Monsieur she'd ordered and gulped at a can of beer fiddling with the TV to see if he could find the BBC News channel.

We may as well be at home in the lounge with our slippers on and no conversation, she thought sadly. There would be no chance of living the high life in Paris tonight. She undressed in the bathroom and slipped under the white crisp sheets in bed hoping he'd soon be joining her.

When she heard him start to snore with his head lolled back on the chair she got up and placed the bedspread over him. He looked exhausted and his usual cheery bright face was drained of all colour. She stared at his face knowing every single line and blemish. She sighed, where was the man she'd loved all her life? Where was the upbeat funny guy who could make her laugh no matter what problems they faced?

The following morning, she woke and felt him behind her in bed. He must have woken through the night and climbed in next to her. Filled with a sense of optimism she threw the covers back and ordered breakfast. The sun streamed through the balcony doors and she opened them intending to have their coffee and croissants at the round table.

She drank her coffee and held her face up to the sunshine while Peter sat opposite in his pyjamas staring ahead at The Eiffel Tower. 'Ah, Parisian croissants and coffee, how lovely,' she said.

He looked down and fiddled with the small packet of butter. 'Look, Angela, I just need to do one quick conference call at ten,' he said and crunched the croissant. 'And, then I'm all yours and we can get out and about to enjoy the sights?'

Angela took a deep breath. She knew there was no point in arguing because it was his work and important to him. 'Okay, I'll meander over to the tower and meet you there, around 11am?'

He nodded and started scrolling down the messages on his mobile.

***

She didn't want to buy the tickets to go up to the top until he joined her, so she strolled around to the front of the Tower's big stretched iron legs. There was only a small queue for tickets with it being early May, but Angela knew in the summer months the line of people would be miles long. She crossed over the road and stood on the end of the Jena Bridge looking over to the right bank with the sun shining on her face.

She remembered them running across the bridge when they were here in their twenties and smiled. Peter had bet her that he could run faster than her and she'd taken up the challenge and beat him. 'I purposely ran slower to let you win,' he'd said grinning.

She heard a wolf-whistle and spun around. The young man opening the small café and souvenir shop grinned towards her and she looked behind to see who he was whistling at. There was only an old man with a stick and a young guy pushing a buggy. Her spirits lifted knowing the whistle was intended for her. Turning back to cross the road she couldn't help sashaying past him in her white jeans.

Angela looked at her watch and skirted the outer glass perimeter to the tower looking for Peter. Where was he? It was half past eleven and he should have ended his call by now? She retraced her steps to the end of the road where the hotel was situated and could feel herself getting annoyed. Of course, the outside surroundings of the tower were different to when they'd been here previously, but, all the same, she seethed walking back to the ticket office, he should be here with her.

She wondered if she should go back to the hotel room and find out if he was still talking to his colleagues but decided to wait. Hanging around for another ten minutes stoked her temper. Was he going to turn up at all? Some romantic meet-cute this had turned out to be, she raged, and then she heard a text ping onto her phone.

'Where are you? I'm in the Trocadero gardens at the front of the tower?'

Angela was furious and stomped off down to the gardens. By the time she reached him sitting calming on a bench with his face held up to the sun, seemingly without a care in the world, she snapped. 'Where the hell have you been?'

A look of weariness entered his eyes and he sighed. 'I thought you'd said to meet at the front of the tower, and this is the front, isn't it?'

'Well,' she huffed. 'Technically I suppose it is, but the ticket office is around the side where I've been waiting for over half an hour!'

He nodded and shrugged his shoulders. 'Oh right, so you want to go up to the top of the tower?'

'Well, yes,' she said and slumped down on the edge of the bench next to him. 'I thought' you'd want to because we did when we came here before?'

'Heavens, Angela, I can't remember what I had for dinner yesterday never mind what we did forty years ago!'

She wrenched the strap of her bag from her shoulder. 'Yeah, well, I guess that's the difference between us, Peter. Because I can. And, I'd hoped this trip might just rekindle things between us because quite frankly, I'm struggling to see the point of us anymore!'

'What!' He swung around to face her.

She raised her voice. 'Peter, since Christmas we've hardly talked to each other at all! Other than the day you told me that the thought of being retired at home horrifies you!'

'Well, I don't think I actually said that?'

Her hands were trembling, and she clasped them tightly together. 'And, when was the last time we actually spent any time together?'

She took in a huge breath. There, she'd said it now, all the months of pent up frustration had tumbled out of her.

'Oh, that's not fair, Angela,' he said drawing his bushy eyebrows together. 'You're nearly always working at the Food Bank, especially at weekends when I'm at home.'

Angela sighed and slumped back on the bench. She had been doing more shifts lately because a few volunteers had left. When she'd started the food bank last year it had only been two days a week, and she'd thought in her small way, she was giving something back to their local community. But she had to admit it had taken over lately.

'Well, I've had to, Peter, because it's probably the only thing nowadays that makes me feel good at the end of a day,' she said. 'Being home with you doesn't anymore.'

She frowned at the sound of her own sad words and her temper deflated like a balloon.

She saw his face crumble thinking about what she'd said. He took her hand and laid it on his leg then squeezed it tightly. His blue eyes filled with tears and she knew she'd upset him.

'Okay, well, I've told you how busy at work I've been, but I'll tell you exactly what's been happening in the company,' he said. 'In January they brought in a young whizz-kid and I knew it was to replace me. I've worried that they would finish me before I'm sixty-six and I'd lose out financially. And, I wanted to prove to them that they still need me for my experience…' he paused. She opened her mouth to speak but knew he wasn't finished.

'Well, more than anything else I'd wanted to prove it to myself,' he said. 'And, in Lyon, I've done just that. The whippersnapper had struck up a deal which when I studied everything in the contract would have been a disaster for us. Luckily, I've stopped the deal before signing.'

'But why didn't you tell me all of this was going on, Peter?'

He shrugged. 'Well, you seemed so absorbed in feeding people at the bank and, I didn't want you to worry.'

She sagged now. She was appalled to think they'd grown so far apart he couldn't talk to her. 'But I thought we were okay with money; you'd told me that when I retired?'

He nodded. 'And we are but I would have just liked the extra two years wages to cover us for a rainy day and, to maybe do some long-haul holidays abroad. I know you've always wanted to visit Australia.'

She knew even if they'd been bankrupt, he would have made her retire and look after her health. She swallowed a lump in her throat.

He sighed. 'But you've always been okay without me at home because you're so independent and well, you just seem to cope with everything life throws at us.

I mean, look how you got Kate through her divorce while I stood by helpless to do anything,' he said. 'I didn't think you needed me all of the time, Angela?'

She felt tears prick at her eyes. 'But I do, Peter,' she said. 'I do need you with me, look at how you helped me through the panic attacks? I couldn't have done that without you.'

He cocked his head. 'Yeah, well, that's the first time in our marriage that you'd lent on me. And, you know, I quite liked holding you up for a change. I felt wanted and was so glad to help *my teacher* when she was struggling,' he teased. 'I'd never seen your vulnerable side before?'

When they'd first met, he'd always called her, *his teacher*, and she smiled at the memory. She melted and threw herself into his big arms.

He hugged her tightly. 'I'm sorry for shutting you out, darling.'

'Oh, Peter, I've felt so alone,' she said. 'At one stage I worried that you'd met someone else?'

He ran his hand through her hair and sighed. 'Never! You're the only one for me, Angela.'

She loved the feel of his hand in her hair it was so soothing, and she felt her whole body relax against him.

'But, you know, Angela, if I'm perfectly honest, I have felt this trip was too much. I'm dog tired of it all now. And, maybe the board are right? As much as I don't want to admit it, I'm struggling to find my usual gusto,' he said. 'Maybe, I should wrap up work now?'

Angela stroked his shoulder. 'Well, Peter, only you will know when the time is right. And, as for money, we'll manage. We don't always have to have expensive holidays like being here in Paris. Being home and together is enough for me?'

He kissed the top of her hair. 'Me, too. And, you know, on that train last night all I could think about was getting here to you.

You're what keeps me sane, Angela,' he said and shivered. 'I've been such an idiot, and to think I nearly lost you!'

She looked up to him and he kissed her. The kiss seemed to last forever. It was how it had always been between them and she knew they were going to be okay.

'So,' he murmured. 'How about we pretend we're twenty-three again and head up that Eiffel Tower to look out over Paris?'

***

Later that night, Angela was sitting opposite him in the restaurant in her pink dress. The small intimate room was full of people laughing, talking, and obviously enjoying the good food. She inhaled the predominant smell of garlic and smiled in contentment.

They'd ordered from the menu and he had a paper serviette in front of him with his pen. 'So, let's make a bucket list of all the places we'd like visit when I retire in August.'

She grinned. 'Great idea, and I've done a little thinking of my own when I was in the shower. I'm going to drop back my hours at the Food Bank to the original two days a week.'

Peter winked at her. 'Okay, Angela the great provider. That's how I always think of you at the food bank telling everyone how to rustle up tasty healthy meals from the few ingredients they have.'

She smiled. 'Bless them, very often it's only beans on toast!'

The waiter brought them bowls of steaming garlic mussels. 'Em, have I told you that tonight you look as delicious as these mussels?'

She still felt warm and contented from their love-making that afternoon. She giggled and ran her shoe up the side of his trouser leg. 'Nope, I don't think you have.'

'Well, I'm loving that dress and the heels, in fact, I can't wait to take them off later!'

Susan Willis

Names.

There are names and names mostly to us in human form portrayed.

Yet, there are other names set in marble, stone or glade.

Serried ranks in perfect order: name, rank, and unit.

On giant edifice, or little meadow, gazing down from dizzy height, or standing alone, on a single stone in the night.

To read a line is to rekindle a memory, the few short phrases but scant record, of what once was a man who shared our world, and went out into it, leaving all the familiar things behind.

Went out into the world abandoning the shining lights, the smells of home, the hearth's delights - never to return.

At first, they were abandoned in foreign fields, visited only by ardent comrades, or, determined kin.

Yet now the world has changed and thousands flock to their stone monuments, or individual spaces.

Fine young faces mouth the words of their name, allowing them to conquer the bugs, the beetles, and thus find a measure of cold immortality, in a cement line of words - a name.

Barry Ross

A Radio Interview

Hi, all you Guys and Gals out there. Welcome to today's show.
Today this is Radio Ninety-Nine's Teenager Help Line, on 1234
Mega Wave, where you are invited to call us with all your
personal problems. Our counsellors will try to help you with
your problems, and we try to offer suitable advice where we
can.

Our first caller is Chelsea. So, Chelsea, you think you might be
pregnant?

I think I'll pass you on to Nurse Catherine, she should be able
to help you. Stay on the line Chelsea. We will talk to you later.

Our next caller is John. Tell me your problem, John.

You know, John, sometimes parents have problems too. It may
be that your parents will get back together again. The only
advice I can give is to carry on loving them equally and just
hope they will see the error of their ways. Thanks, for the call,
John, I hope matters get sorted soon, keep listening.

Hello, Mark, how can Radio Ninety-Nine help you? Have you
any grandparents in your area, Mark.

Well then, I would go to talk to them about your mothers
drinking. Does your father know about her problem?

Oh, I'm sorry about that. Perhaps that is why she has turned to
drink. I would definitely talk to your grandparents. Good luck,
Mark.

On the line now is Sophie. Good morning, Sophie, how can we
help you?

If your friends are saying that you should have sex with your
boyfriend, then they certainly are not good friends. How old are
you, Sophie?

My advice, Sophie, is to trust your own conscience. When you,
and not just your boyfriend, are ready for sex, your own body
and mind will tell you. And please make sure that you protect
yourself. Perhaps a word with your doctor might help.

Welcome back, Chelsea, has Nurse Catherine been able to help you?

That's good. Thanks for your call, Chelsea and the very best of luck to you and your baby.

Now we welcome, Tom, to the show. How can we help you, Tom?

Thinking you might be different is not the same as being different. Perhaps waiting until you are a little older will give you the chance to be sure. Thanks for your call, Tom, and now we have Jennie on the line.

It is an interesting question that you pose, Jennie. That is outside my knowledge. Can I pass you on to Nurse Catherine and I'll speak to you later?

Welcome to the show, Adam, please tell me why you have called.

May I ask how old you are, Adam?

Adam, your boss should not be employing a boy of your age full time. So, the rate of pay for such work is not in question here. He may give you small tasks to do as odd jobs, for a nominal payment. Both he and you could be in trouble if it became known that you were employed full time.

Now we have time for just one more question before we go into a short break.

Hello, Jimmy.

That is quite a problem you have, Jimmy, can I mull this over during the commercial break? Stay on the line and we'll be back in a couple of ticks.

Sorry to keep you waiting, Jimmy. So, Jennie is your girlfriend?

We think that you are both still quite young to be engaging in full sex. There are other ways that you can enjoy each other's minds and bodies. I am sure Nurse Catherine will be discussing these with your girlfriend now. Thanks for the call. It helps a lot when we can advise both parties in a relationship.

And now we have Barry on the line. Thanks for calling, Barry.

I am very sorry, Barry, but Newcastle United and England football are outside the scope of this programme, although they could do with loads of advice. Perhaps we could have a phone-in about these problems in the near future? Barry, you sound quite mature. Are you aware that this is a phone-in for teenagers? Now, our next teenage caller is Samantha. Tell me your problem Samantha?

That is a sad tale, I am sorry for you, Samantha. Right, I'll call you, Sam then. How do you think we can help you, Sam?

We are not qualified to advise you here, Sam. I think you should report that to the police. Good luck.

Hello, John, good of you to call back.

That is good news. Your parents have decided to get back together. So glad we could help. Keep listening.

Next on the line is Robbie from Sunderland, how can we help Robbie?

You have split your sides through laughing? I think you are trying to send a message here Robbie. And you do not sound like a teenager. You should call our football phone-in after 6pm, perhaps you may have bled to death by then.

Look lads and lasses, this is not a phone-in for mad football fanatics. For that you will need to call the asylum.

After wasting time on idiotic football fans, I think there is just time for one more quick call.

Hello, Mary, how can I help you? My dinner is on the table? I'll be home in five minutes. Goodbye, folks, and don't forget to tune into Radio Ninety-Nine tomorrow when we will be talking about marital problems.

Harry Mason

I'm From Gateshead

Where are YOU from?
They would ask you (as an opening line)
The 1950s answer was,
"Newcastle upon Tyne"

In the 60s – more explicit –
but still avoiding hassle,
the answer you might give them was,
"Gateshead, near Newcastle"

In the 70s they knew Gateshead
because Carter (Michael Caine)
threw that fella off the car park roof
(no one dies in vain)

Then of course, there was the Stadium
Brendan Forster, Great North Run.
"Oh, yes, Gateshead" they'd say, vaguely,
well we'd only just begun!

In the 80s we got 'culture'
Art and more art was the cry.
So this mix of sport and sculpture
ended up (oh why? Oh why?)
in that fat bloke on the West Street
with his crunchy tortoise pie.

But, of course, the Metro Centre
was the 80s golden spur
to bring the people flocking in
(and some knew where they were!)

It was thought regeneration
was in order, truth to tell
and the 90s Garden Festival
began the decade well.
But the thing that made us famous
and a place of great renown
was in 1998
when the Angel came to town!

Then everyone had heard of us,
Broadsheets, Tabloids and TV.
We were showered with attention
through 'Angelic' intervention
and you only had to mention
where you came from and you'd see
on the face of the enquirer,
full and utter comprehension.

What comes next? The year 2000!
We'll hold our heads up high.
A concert hall, an arts centre,
we're aiming for the sky!

Just say "Gateshead" when they ask you
where you're from (take it from me)
They'll say "Isn't that fantastic!
Gateshead's where we all should be!"

Maureen C Bell

The Trafficker's Tale

I've had to trample on people to get to the top in my line of business.

Money makes our world go around. Everyone's the same from that point of view. When you hear stories about trafficking gone wrong, that is when we are found out because the travellers die or escape, there's a TV debate about how people can do this. 'That poor dead child washed up on the beach,' they say. 'People suffocating in a locked lorry.' The communal scratching of heads and wringing of hands.

Well it's easy. I'm just a facilitator.

People and their families want to move into richer countries. I help them achieve that. I sort out their journeys, you know, a kind of travel agent, sorting out my steps of their itinerary. I carry all the risk which is why my commission is high. Burner phones cost money. Sourcing boats and pilots. That's what we call them. It's a tricky job. We give them training. Once they have the big stick, those without their own gun, all they need to do is maintain order and wear their own lifejackets. The ones we really rate, we give wet suits. Once they land safely, I take over. If they're caught or the boat develops a problem, know how to create a diversion when the authorities arrive. A medical emergency on board is always good, then they run for it, or look for the jet ski if we know what's happening and can help them out. They need to keep themselves safe for the next time.

Self-preservation, that's the key.

At first some of the pilots don't like to beat the fathers who are frightened their children are going to drown, or who ask for answers, fresh water, protection from the rain. The first beating is the worst. They may have been doctors, judges, architects in their previous lives these travellers, but on our boats, they are all damp bundles of cash. Causing trouble- it's unsafe, not good for the risk assessment. It's put up or shut up in my business. A straight choice, but not everyone sees it that way.

They're the ones who end up going over.

The last one we put over could've been an Olympic standard swimmer, a really feisty guy. Still, after a few chilly Med minutes, that's what we like to call them, when the torch was passed over the dark water he'd given up. His wife was whimpering, shushing their baby. My business associate said the mother and daughter would end up at the house on Shore Street. They were the right age. The baby would be re-homed. They should think themselves lucky. They could have gone over the side with dear 'ol Papa.

No money-back guarantees here.

What happens when they leave my care is not my problem. I spend no time thinking about it. I look at the bottom line of my bank account at the end of every day and kiss the screen of my iPhone. That's my god, the dollars, the euros, the pounds.

What makes me good at my job?

I have lived that journey, known the terror of that crossing. We were lucky to make it unscathed, but as the master walked down to the shore issuing destinations for my family, I passed out. We'd had nothing to eat for three days. So, they checked me, left me on the ground to recover. But I heard them. Sending my Mama to work for the gang-master's wife, helping with their children. My sister to the den, my brothers to the fruit farmer. If they'd known about me, I mean, the real me…well, that makes me shudder.

I ran 'til my legs became solid, leaden. There was a church. The priest took me in. His housekeeper liked me. She fed me gnocchi and we talked about where I was from. We hit a bump in the road when she started to ask about my age. I overheard her asking the priest, did he know I was fifteen? He'd need to involve the authorities because I was a victim of crime, she said.

The result was another dodgy journey, but once the Italian police were shaken off, I made it to England in the back of a refrigerated lorry.

It cost me, that journey, when I had no money. I walked every street, scoped out the town, visited everywhere I could to find people like me. A cardboard bed under the railway arches was my home until the research was done. Nail bars, pubs, takeaways. I'd ask for the boss, say I was seeking work. I looked young, good-looking.

Vulnerable.

I'd find out everything, language, background, were they legitimate? Once we'd spoken, I'd ask for the toilet. And run. I could always clock a good time around the track.

I worked out who was too dangerous. Who had their own prejudices, desires? That's how I ended up with my business associate. He was young and clever too. He still had contacts back home. He locates the punters, the pilots, the craft. We had to watch the news, research, best methods to move people. RHIBs, he said. They're good, light and strong, easy to get your hands on without leaving a trail. Big payload too.

What we can't control- the dark, the sea. Finding your way across open water- we tried it once. Acknowledge your skillset, know what you're good at. We leave that to others now.

Money collections and arranging the Welcoming Committee shore side, that's my part of the deal. And the advice from Uncle. He helped us get going. He has good links and lets us know if things are getting a little too close.

My Mama and Papa always wanted the best for me, knew I'd get to the top in business somewhere.

I'm not sure they'd approve, but wherever they are, I would say this is 'full circle'

Alwyn Bathan

It's the Morning After Our Last Meeting

"Let's have a five-day break in Rome," Louise said excitedly.

"Oooh, yes we've not been there, all that history," I said.

"All those gorgeous Italian men," she giggled.

A few weeks later we stepped off the plane, eventually we arrived at our hotel. We had to enter an old-fashioned iron lift, the sort you would find in the godfather film. Two floors up and we were in our clean room, traditional with a huge modern bathroom. The windows looked out on a small courtyard, ordained with flowers and plants.

"Let's unpack then we can explore the area and have a nice coffee," I said.

Half an hour later we walked out into the warm sunshine. The plaza was buzzing with people, artists were trying to sell their beautiful paintings to tourists. The smell of food filled the air. We had our photo taken by a fountain, then headed over to a small busy restaurant. Locals were sitting outside under the red and white candy-striped canopy.

"Let's sit over there," I pointed. We ordered two large glasses of wine, then looked through the menu.

"What are you having," I asked Louise.

"Pizza or pasta we're in Italy," she laughed.

Our food was delicious, the atmosphere was great. Just sitting listening to the Italians made it more so. Louise and I chatted and relaxed by watching the world go by. We laughed at tourists bartering with stall holders and were intrigued by priests and nuns hurrying down the plaza.

"Senoras," the waiter said as he placed two glasses of wine on the table.

"Oh, we haven't ordered those," I said.

He said something in Italian, smiled and gestured to the table behind us. We turned around at the same time.

Sitting behind us were two gorgeous Italian men. They raised their glasses in the air.

"Wow!" Louise smiled.

"Gratzi," we chorused.

"Can we join you," one of them said in broken English.

"Of course, you can if you're buying drinks," Louise laughed.

Seconds later we were introduced to Giovani and Tomaso. Tomaso chatted to Louise, they laughed as they tried to communicate with the language barrier. Giovani on the other hand, spoke a little better English. He was around six foot two, with black curly shoulder length hair. His dark smouldering eyes seemed to light up when he spoke. A gold hoop earring hung from one ear. His tanned masculine face was perfect, very handsome, I thought, he definitely ticked all of my boxes. Even the clothes he wore was sexy. Tight white jeans and a pale blue shirt revealing a tanned smooth chest.

"Let's move on," Louise gestured. Finishing our drinks, we paid our bill and left the restaurant with the two Italians following behind. The guys took us to their local bars.

"I want to dance," I shouted over the music to Louise.

Taking my hand Giovani led me on to the dance floor. His dance moves were incredible. It was after midnight when Louise and I decided to call it a night.

"Tomaso wants to show us the sights tomorrow if you fancy it?" We agreed a time and place to meet.

The next morning after breakfast, we went off to meet Tomaso, my heart skipped a beat when I saw Giovani standing beside him. The sights were incredible, we were in awe of The Trevi Fountain. The sculptures and statues carved by men all those years ago, and the mighty colosseum took our breath away, this fabulous city was steeped in history. We stopped for lunch, then carried on to the Vatican. We were totally blown away, Michael Angelo, enormous statues everywhere you turned. Giovani and Tomaso were so proud.

"My feet are killing me," Louise moaned. "Ow I've got a blister; we'll have to go back to the hotel."

Jumping into a taxi we headed back. Giovani gestured for me to go and have a drink in a bar not far from our hotel. Smiling at Louise, she said it was fine she was going to bathe her poor feet. I told her I wouldn't be late.

We sat and enjoyed each other's company: Giovani was charismatic and very charming. But it was getting very late, and the alcohol was taken its toll.

"Time to go," I laughed.

"My home is not far," he pointed. "Coffee?"

Mesmerised by his handsome face. I said, "Yes."

His apartment was lovely and spacious.

"Just milk," I said as I went off to find the toilet. While I was in there, I text Louise.

"See you in the morning," she texted back.

"I'll be back soon," I texted back.

I found Giovani sitting on the sofa, with two large glasses of wine.

"Oh, I think I've had enough to drink," I gestured.

"To us," he said in his sexy accent.

"To us," I smiled.

Giovani's gorgeous eyes bore into mine; I felt a bit embarrassed and looked away. I felt his hand on my face, slowly he turned my face towards him. Then moved forward and gently kissed my lips. God he's so sexy I thought as I drank my wine. Refilling our glasses, Giovani took me by the hand and lead me on to his veranda. I knew I'd had too much to drink, but I was enjoying his company. Once outside the fresh air hit me like a thunderbolt.

The sun was shining through the blinds, I squinted my eyes. Then suddenly it dawned on me this wasn't my hotel room.

"Oh Christ," I thought. I cautiously looked under the duvet cover, all I had on was my underwear.

I was totally confused; I couldn't remember a thing. How I got to bed, undressed or anything. My head felt like a sledgehammer.

Louise, I thought, she must be worried sick. The bedroom door opened Giovani appeared carrying a tray with coffee and croissants.

"Morning," he smiled. I quickly sat up; he gave me the tray. Then got into bed beside me. My mind was racing, I frantically tried to remember what happened last night. Slowly I remembered being on the veranda, then my mind went blank.

"Giovani what happened last night?" I asked.

"We didn't, you know?" I glanced at him. How I wished we could get over the language barrier.

Giovani realised what I was trying to say, "No," he said. "Respecto."

Feeling guilty, I quickly dressed, and hurried back to the hotel. I quietly opened the door; Louise was still asleep. Thank God I thought. Five minutes later I stepped out of the shower, popped the kettle on. Then made Louise her breakfast.

"Morning sleepy head, how's your feet," I said.

"What time did you get in," Louise asked.

"Not sure, but I've got a splitting headache," I frowned.

"Where's your breakfast?"

"I've already eaten," I said looking away.

"Can we spend the rest of our holiday just the two of us together," I said.

"I was hoping you were going to say that, we'll be going home soon," Louise replied.

***

"Can you believe, Louise, we were in Rome just over a month ago?"

"I know," she sighed. Tomaso hasn't texted for over two weeks now. "What time is your doctor's appointment," she said sipping her coffee.

"2 o'clock, my blood test should be back. I just feel so tired since we've come back."

"Let me know how you get on?"

"Miss Harrington, would you like to come through," the nurse smiled. "Your blood test is back; I hope congratulations are in order?"

Mandy Baharie

Sherlock Holmes

I am an old man now, alone in a cottage near Surrey,
I take each day as it comes; there is no need to hurry,
I lost my dear wife Mary, nearly four years ago.
She died of consumption, a death painful and slow,
For me a Doctor of Medicine, it was hard to watch Mary die,
She bore her pain bravely, losing all strength to try,
We never had children, but we were happy we two,
Our marriage a perfect match, our arguments few,
She supported my work, though I caused her much strife,
She was indeed patient, my loving darling wife,
For many long months, she did not know where I had gone,
My work took me to strange places, the hours were long,
Medicine was my profession, but my interests were more
diverse,
A biographer and detective's associate, a veritable curse,

The detective in question, Sherlock Holmes was his
designation,
A friend of over forty years, a sleuth of legendary oration,
My life was entwined with Sherlock, and his brilliant brain,
No case has eluded him, treating criminals with disdain,
Moriarty considered, he had a superior criminal mind,
Holmes, he tried to outmanoeuvre, but his ambition was blind,
Sherlock Holmes caused his demise, in a fight to the death,
Moriarty cursed the detective, with his last dying breath,
A woman impressed him; Irene Adler was her name,
Her crime was near perfect, she put Sherlock to shame,
The Metropolitan Police, recognised Holmes for his skill,
Inspector Lestrude relied on him, leading him to the kill,
My role next to Sherlock, was to document each crime,
Millions have read his exploits, a legend captured in time,

Holmes retired to Sussex, of Bees he became a Keeper,
Awaiting the day, he would meet his grim reaper,
I corresponded with him by letter, we reminisced on the past,
The detection of criminality, our memories were vast,
He enjoyed the sea views; he walked and took the air,
A pillar in the community, an enigma they could share,
But then I received a letter, an invitation to stay with my friend,
A chance for us to walk together, my acceptance I did send,
I arrived on the Sunday, Holmes was attentive and alert,
Though he did seem rather preoccupied, his responses curt,
Soon I realised I had been summoned, to help solve a crime,
He asked if I had brought my revolver, all would be revealed in time,
I should have known from experience, the invitation was a rouse,
Sherlock Holmes was embroiled in an adventure, with little time to lose,

A local landowner's son, had fallen from a cliff face,
The death was potentially a suicide, of murder there was no trace,
But Holmes was not certain, that all was as it appeared,
He was convinced of wrongdoing, his suspicions I feared,
He searched the whole area, examining the scene,
He questioned the witnesses, establishing where they had been,
I sensed he already knew, the perpetrator of the crime,
Not yet ready to share his findings, he needed more time,
To his violin he turned, playing long into the night,
He smoked his precious opium, looking a harrowing sight,
However, as the dawn broke, there was a light in his eye,
He knew the identity of the killer, he had seen through the lie,
The murderer was the father; he had sacrificed his second son,
To secure the family business, the deed had to be done,

The father was arrested, the hangman's noose he did face,
But he did not regret his actions; he had yet one ace,
His first son would inherit, the business and its wealth,
He would continue like his father, managing with stealth,
Without father or brother, the son would not prosper it was
clear,
He sunk into depression, he had lost those dear,
The first-born took his life; the whole family were lost,
The sins of the father, had enacted their cost,
Of my holiday this is my story, with my dearest friend,
It seems even in Sussex, his sleuthing would never end,
We enjoyed the few days remaining, discussing our deeds,
Holmes was at his most articulate, neglecting all my needs,
We were old men now, no longer up to the chase,
For Sherlock Holmes and Dr Watson, retirement we must face,

Maria Barrell

The Blaydon Races
Come and see the Blaydon Races
Fun for one and all
Pack a basket full of goodies
And come and have a ball
It may get a little raucous
Someone might burst into song
But that's all part of the pleasure
So join in with the throng!

Bring a little money if you have some
As a sweet stall is there to delight
Keep any children close by you
In case the lads start a fight
You will see many colourful characters
Like a clown, a jester and his dog
Beware of the many pickpockets
As they're very good at their job!

At the end of the day as sun sets
As you tread your weary way home
Head still buzzing with all the excitement
Feet feeling like they've turned to stone
Your heart and mind will never tire
Of bringing memories to the fore
That day you spent at the races
Blaydon - the best you ever saw!

Tracey Monaghan

The Horror Of Haribo's

'Mum! The social worker has told you not to go on your phone,' Elsie said.

She glowered at her mother. It was her fault they were here.

'If Billy sees you're online, he could find out where we are.'

She walked across to the window and tried to look beyond the condensation that sat between the glass panes. Down the garden, overturned wheelie bins disgorged their contents on the scrubby grass. It could be worse, she thought. Someone had sprayed the word *PEDO* in yellow paint across the windows of the house opposite.

'Are you listening, Mum?' she checked, using her fingernail to extract black mould lodged around the frames. It was like the windows in the science lab at school. Elsie hated her new school. And her new 'friends' who looked down their noses at her, the 'needy' one, the 'poor' one. Whether it was second-hand uniform, 'donated' from the new school's pastoral team or leftovers from PE sinbin, it didn't help.

They all knew, of course. But no-one had said it yet. Or called her the usual names.

But there was time to come.

Elsie knew that other parents, the ones who cared and were skilled at planning, arranged for their children to swap schools at the start of the academic year, or the term, or even just after they'd moved house. But they'd never have their child turn up to their new school on a Wednesday morning looking like they'd been dragged out of bed in the dark, had the contents of their top drawer stuffed into a black bin bag and turned out a day later in someone else's donated and crumpled uniform. On her first day, the armpits of her school shirt had been crusty, and she smelled of someone else's sweat.

Elsie was going to make certain it would be a new start.

It was two whole weeks since they'd left their house on Macmillan Street.

Overnight, Elsie had lost her own bedroom, lost the rest of their family, lost her friends. Now, was about keeping.

Keeping her mother from Billy.

Keeping themselves safe.

'It'll be fine,' Becky said, her face still illuminated by the screen. 'We're miles away now. He doesn't know where we live. I've just given Nan the bus number to get here.'

Elsie smiled.

She'd love to see Nan.

'It's the 72 that stops at the end of the street, isn't it?'

Nan had stepped in when Mum was absent. She'd read them stories when Mum was out clubbing with Billy. She'd cooked their suppers while Mum was helping Billy peddle his wares, and Nan had put clean sheets on their beds when Billy's friends took over the house and slept in their beds. Nan was the one who bought fresh boxes of Frosty Snowflakes to replace the ones they'd eaten, and she'd even bought Neil a new PlayStation when his was broken during that punch-up.

'I've told her to make sure there's no-one around as she leaves the house. Once she's on the bus, she'll be fine,' Becky said.

Nan would bring a big bag.

Nappies for the baby.

Ciggies for Becky.

Sanitary towels for Elsie.

Haribo's for Neil.

Becky sent one last message.

CHECK ROUND WHEN YOU LEAVE. TAKE CARE. XXX

Elsie ran upstairs.

'Neil, guess who's on her way?'

'Ooh! Haribo's!' he squealed. He ran in circles around the tiny bedroom with his arms stretched out like an aeroplane, crashing into everything around him. 'It's been ages since I had them!'

As she settled the baby to a feed, Becky rested her phone on the arm of the chair. They took turns to watch the digital minutes increase, start again, and increase toward Nan's arrival.

She congratulated herself on leaving the house and getting on the bus without being seen by anyone. Nan had looked very carefully, squinted even, to make sure there was no-one around as she walked to the bus stop.

A future career as a spy, she mused. Middle aged women could pass anywhere, everyone knew that. Turning 50 brought powers of invisibility.

She'd been looking for people, not the silver Subaru Impreza parked further down Pitt Street.

As the number 72 pulled away from the bus stop, fumes fired inside the car's twin exhausts.

The bus chugged its route to Risebrough, stopping every 5 minutes. Nan lost count of the number of stops, but the unfamiliar territory brought a change to her expression. They passed gardens full of water-logged sofas. A pack of dogs ran across the road bringing the bus to a momentary halt. No-one alighted at the next stop.

Four flat tyres supported what was left of a black BMW.

Getting off the bus at the art deco Ritz cinema, now painted purple as the Regal bingo, the grannie swapped the heavy carrier bag from one hand to the other. Her fingertips first turned red, then blue, to white. Finding the door, she was looking for, she pulled the bag close to her and rattled the worn letterbox cover.

Inside the house, Becky shouted to Elsie and Neil, telling them to pull the curtains. Make sure nothing could be seen by the neighbours, she said. They ran around, checking there were no gaps to be seen through. What about the blind in the bathroom? they asked. That too. A flurry of movement and excitement filled the house for a few seconds.

Happy voices, hilarity even.

It made Becky smile, remembering how happy the children could be.

Together, they stood in their line, Becky holding the sleeping baby in front of her. Elsie reached up to release the safety chain. She pulled the door open and the three looked out, their faces poised in happy expectation.

There was no Nan was on the doorstep.

Just a blue and yellow carrier bag, the contents of which had been strewn across the already unkempt front garden. Haribo's, nappies and sanitary towels scattered amongst the weeds, litter and mud.

Lying open, the tobacco sticks shredded, a note had been scribbled on the back of the cigarette packet. YOU'RE NEXT.

Alwyn Bathan

Jigsaw

James McDonald Curtis placed the final piece of the final jigsaw into the last perfect vacant shape waiting to receive it. He looked at his right hand still hovering over the completed picture of the New York skyline, noted the dry skin, the blue raised veins, the enlarged joints. "Has it all been worth it?" he wondered, but before he could decide the matter his spirit left his body and he pitched forward onto the table, scattering jigsaw pieces across the dark, swirly patterned carpet.

"Police or Ambulance?" Avril wondered. It was a fairly rhetorical question as she didn't think Dulce would have much idea.

"How long do you think he's been, ye know, like that?"

"Dead you mean" Avril answered. Dulce winced at the word, her eyes filling.

"Well, he was alright on Monday when we were here, so not more than two days."

"Should we get on, do you think? Will we be in trouble?"

"You pop upstairs and start on the bathroom." It would keep Dulce occupied. "I'll phone the police."

"No," both women told the police officer. "Mr Curtis never mentioned any family."

"No," they agreed. "No one ever called, not when they were there."

"All Mr Curtis did," they added, "was to leave them to get on with their work, cleaning, dusting, vacuuming, polishing the windows, changing the nets, all that sort of thing. Then he would give Avril his shopping list for a week's groceries. He always had the money ready for the shopping and their pay. Apart from that all they ever saw him do was jigsaw puzzles."

"Why two of you," the police officer wanted to know.

"Dulce, love, make us a cup of tea."

Avril winked at the policeman and when Dulce went off to the kitchen Avril explained that she looked after her younger sister who, 'wasn't quite the ticket.'

Mr Curtis had asked to meet her and then told Avril she could bring her along to help. "I was so grateful to him and she really is a great help if I tell her what to do."

The police officer told them he would want to see them again and they could go home now.

Mrs Curtis, now Zoe Beaumont, was contacted after a long search. James McDonald Curtis and Zoe had never divorced. He would never have done so willingly, and she didn't see the need to bother. She simply reverted to her maiden name and carried on with her life.

"So, the miserable old so and so has gone, has he," she thought when she received the solicitor's letter. "I wonder if he made a will?"

"We're still married, you know," she told her latest love. "And he has no relatives. He had only one sister, Audrey, and she wasn't the full shilling. Come to think of it," she laughed, "neither was he. Him and his jigsaw puzzles."

Jake yawned. He wasn't interested in her past, some of which had occurred before he was born but when she told him about the house, he took more interest.

Zoe couldn't sleep that night. Jake was snoring away as she crept downstairs to think about her short and unexciting marriage to James. With a cup of tea and a slice of toast and raspberry jam before her, she considered her position when she had married him.

She just had to get married. There was no alternative. To her mother, grandmother and aunts, being married was what girls did. None of this 'moving in.' This was bred in her bones.

When Richard Barnes dropped her, and here she muttered darkly and bit hard into her toast, it was imperative that she saved face and found someone else without delay.

At this point James McDonald Curtis wandered across her line of sight. A quiet, gentle man of about 40, he lived alone. His 'mad sister' as Zoe referred to her lived with her aunt Jane, his deceased mother's sister. James would have been broken hearted when Audrey died, she thought. She knew how much he loved his sister, which annoyed her when they were together.

Although seventeen years her senior, James didn't stand a chance. Zoe was determined to be married and he had a decent job as an accountant, he had a house left to him by his, fortunately, deceased parents, he was tall, not bad looking and she felt she could make something of him.

Zoe pretended to enjoy classical concerts, lectures at the Lit & Phil, even jigsaw puzzles, thinking 'I will change him when we are married.' James pretended nothing and did not change after marriage. He considered himself happy at first but became more and more bewildered as his 'loving little girl' turned into a raging virago out of sheer boredom. Above all she hated the jigsaw puzzles.

When he invited her to 'find all the edge pieces first, darling' she imagined the immense satisfaction she would derive from plunging the carving knife into his heart. Practical soul that she was, however, she decided to improve her life in other ways and, not being a woman to take up flower arranging or pottery, she took to adultery with alacrity. Soon she left James and went through a series of lovers over the years, the present one being Jake who, it has to be said, was a step down-market from many of her previous soulmates.

She sighed. With time her choices had narrowed. Probably Jake was the end of the line, she would have to hang onto him. He had a job of sorts and she had a pension from work. They were okay, but a legacy wouldn't go wrong and she was, after all, next of kin.

Pushing the last bit of toast and raspberry jam into her mouth, Zoe began to laugh, almost choking herself, as she thought of the day, she had told James she was leaving him.

"But we're married," James stuttered, looking completely bewildered, "you can't be having…" he flushed searching for a word, "you can't be having relations with a man. That would be adultery?"

"Of course, it's adultery, idiot!" Zoe screamed, wanting to shake him, "and Eddie's not the first, and I am not remotely sorry, and…"

"I certainly made quite a speech," Zoe thought.

James' problem was his difficulty believing this was happening to him. He simply did not know how to react. Should he shout, should he threaten to punch Eddie, should he slap Zoe, should he offer to forgive her, what should he do? He stared at her, more shocked than he had ever been in his life. When he suddenly felt tears threatening to spill down his face, he turned and walked out of the room and out of the house into the garden.

"He started pruning the roses," she told her friend Jan, "can you credit it. I tell him I'm leaving him, and he goes and prunes the roses."

Drinking her tea, and making herself another slice of toast, Zoe remembered her parting 'gift' to James. He had gone to visit his aunt and his dopey sister. "Probably telling them what a harlot I am," she thought.

Her belongings were stacked in the hall waiting for Eddie to collect them. She remembered looking around the living room to see if she had forgotten anything and then glancing into the dining room where the large oak table was constantly occupied by a jigsaw puzzle. One wall was lined with shelves holding rows of neatly lined up boxed puzzles, maybe a couple of hundred, maybe more.

She recalled gleefully the thought which had struck her and how she had begun to grab the boxes off the shelves, tearing them open and pouring out the contents onto the dark swirly-patterned carpet.

She saw her younger self ripping into box after box, then viewing the huge pile of thousands of small shapes. She had dived in among them, grabbing up handfuls and throwing them up into the air.

"What's going on?" Eddie was standing in the doorway. She spun around, glowing, and flung her arms around him. They fell about laughing, hurling jigsaw pieces over each other. Zoe sighed. She had loved Eddie. They had had a great time. Where was he now, she wondered.

Having finished the toast and drained the teapot, and still laughing at her memories, Zoe went back to bed, sliding quietly under the duvet beside the sleeping Jake.

On their way to the solicitor's office the following day, Zoe and Jake speculated on what her inheritance would be.

"The house is Victorian," Zoe told him, "thank goodness I only redecorated and didn't rip out the original features. The garden is huge. It should be worth about £400,000."

"He might have changed it in 30 odd years. Or someone else might have."

"No, not the James I remember. It will be just as I left it. I can't see James with another woman unless he married her, and we were never divorced. No, I think I'm going to do all right out of this."

The solicitor was young and his office bright and bland. After his, "Good morning, Mrs Curtis and Mr....er?" he looked at Jake expectantly.

"Bradley," Zoe informed him. "A friend."

She refused the offer of coffee just wanting to get on with it.

"James McDonald Curtis," he began, "left the bulk of his capital, some £200,000…" he droned on about shares and bonds, "to Avril Somers and Dulce Anderson."

"And who are Avril Somers and Dulce Anderson?" The extremely unlikely vision of a ménage trois popped into Zoe's head. "Never James," she thought smiling to herself.

"The two sisters who have cleaned his house and attended to his laundry and shopping for many, many years while he got on with what was his life's ambition."

"What was his life's ambition?" Zoe was curious.

"It seems that thirty or so years ago, your husband was burgled, and the burglar emptied part of Mr Curtis's collection of jigsaws, somewhere about 90 I believe, into one big heap on the floor. Mr Curtis determined to complete each one and re-box it. In order to accomplish this, he employed Mrs Somers and her sister Miss Anderson to look after his shopping etc. and a Mr Thomas to tend the garden. His time was limited at first but after retirement he devoted his whole energy into sorting out the puzzles. It seems he had just put the last piece in place when his heart gave out."

Zoe stared at the young man. 'Astounded' hardly approached what she was feeling.

"You, Mrs Curtis, have been left the house on the conditions to be found in this letter," he handed her an envelope. "I also have a copy of these conditions. Would you like to read your letter in private?"

Zoe rose from her seat, stunned at the thought of James spending thirty years sorting out that heap of cardboard. She sat with Jake in the small room the solicitor provided, this time accepting the offered coffee and wishing it was something stronger.

"You've got the house anyway, love" Jake ventured, thinking of the new car and the holidays they would have after it was sold.

"Just shut up, Jake, will you. I've a horrible feeling about this." She slid her finger under the flap of the envelope.

Dear Zoe (the letter began)
I bequeath you the house I have lived in my whole life.
There is a condition. You must live in the house. (Zoe pulled a face) *It will not be yours to dispose of until you have restored to order that which you will find on the dining room floor, prepared for you by my solicitor, Andrew Stokes and almost exactly as you left it.*
He will ensure that everything is ready for you to begin. He will periodically check on your progress and mark off each item as you complete it. When all has been restored, the house will be yours to do with as you wish.
The burglary is my small fiction. You and I know the truth.
Should you decide that the task is too great, or is not to your taste, the house will be sold, and the proceeds given to various named charities.
Your husband,
James McDonald Curtis

                          Maureen Bell

Caring Isolation: Diary Extracts

Sunday

It happened once before, two years ago. The illness was insidious; abdominal discomfort, dull pain, weight loss, poor appetite. Is it not strange that the usual becomes common place? I began to own my symptoms, anticipate them; they became a part of me. Someone noticed I was weak, a little disorientated. But these were my symptoms; they were part of me.

Then hospital admission, questions, when did the symptoms start? What symptoms? I had no sense of timing. I was isolated for two weeks in a hospital cubicle. Everyone wore gowns and gloves. I did not recognise my family. I was surrounded by magnolia walls, a small window overlooking a car park. I could see out, but no one could see me. The silence was deafening, no voice.

I lost my symptoms. I came home. I regained myself, experiences faded into my past, a distant memory.

The symptoms have returned, just as insidious. I recognise them, I can manage, they become a part of me. I am back in isolation, magnolia walls, small window overlooking another small window with closed curtains. I can see the curtains, light and dark but nothing can see me.

Visiting is limited; staff come in and out as quickly as possible. I am isolated, I am alone. It is silent. I am thinking but I have no voice. I have got a radio. I like the sound of radio 4. I do not focus on the content, but the sound is soothing, calming, reassuring, normalising.

My symptoms are back with me. I am used to them; they have a history, a memory. I want them to be transient, but I want to remember. I cannot remember the pain. Does pain have a memory? Perhaps not it is just pain and it hurts.

It is day 1 in isolation. I can cope. I organise myself, put away my towel, wash bag, pyjamas. I have juice, books and magazines, my diary. I have my phone, I can text. I am organised in less than ten minutes.

No one comes into isolation unless for a purpose. Hours go by. A nurse comes to record my observations. The Doctor examines me. Treatment is commenced, bloods collected. I am on my own. I have a cup of tea at four hourly intervals. Meals come on trays; I cannot eat. I am isolated.

My family comes dressed in gowns and gloves. After initial pleasantries there is nothing to say. They are in an alien environment, feeling hot, feeling exposed. Why is visiting four hours long? I want a short visit every hour. Perhaps meeting someone else's visitors would be interesting, hearing their stories.

I send my text messages; receive responses and I am alone. I sleep for an hour, read, sleep, read, sleep. There is no distinction between day and night, no pattern.

My symptoms have become my structure; they now define me as a patient, no longer a person. A patient is uncharacteristic; nightwear, no distinguishing features, no voice, a clutch of symptoms. The objectification of the patient. Patients support patients, caring for each other. There is no patient support in isolation. I cannot leave my room. I do not know my fellow patients. I am the isolation patient, alienated by my peers.

Monday

It is just after midnight, I am awake. I have had my medication, observations completed, teeth cleaned, washed and toileted by ten o'clock. Fast asleep then fully awake just after midnight. Disorientated, alone, confused, sad. I am surrounded by magnolia walls. Nothing to see out of the window, only, darkness.

There is noise all around me. The ward is alive in the early hours.

Trolleys rattling, voices raised, shouts of "nurse," "nurse," "please." There are feet running. My door is closed. I am the isolation patent.

No one checks me. I am classified as "no trouble," "suffers in silence," "always pleasant," "no bother." They say my rooms always smells lovely; it always looks cosy.

I fiddle with my back rest and pillows and try to sleep. The noises do not pass my threshold; they stop outside, listen to my silence and move on. I am cubicle 1, isolation.

Time passes; the night comes to an end. My isolation drill starts at 6 o'clock. A nurse records my observations; "no pain, that's good" she says, I ask for clean sheets and change my bed. Shower, teeth cleaned changed. Rice krispies for breakfast, weak tea. It is 7 o'clock, drill complete, "no bother."

Doctor will see me today, decide about treatment, tell me how I feel and what will happen.

Alone again until visitors.

I compare my life at this moment to being a prisoner in isolation. My pyjamas my uniform, my prison pallor, my weak shuffle. The most dangerous are isolated. I am dangerous, I could infect others. I am labelled, I am stereotyped. What do other patients think I look like? I am not allowed out of my room. Do they imagine I am physically scarred, a hideous sight? Do I need a bell, to tell everyone I am near?

My room has no mirror, why is that? But I have my own so I can see myself. I look like me, I know me, I cannot hear me, but I am here. How do I know what I now see is me, my symptoms are part of me, they have become me, they have changed me? This is the new me. My change has evolved, I have not realised. What will happen to the me I knew? Isolation, deterioration, death or recovery,

Oh misery, what will become of me?

Tuesday

An uneventful night I thought. Distant noises, cries in the night. My isolation is interrupted in the semi darkness of the hospital night. I am in a state of semi consciousness, just the night light on in my isolation room. I hear and then slowly recognise the inner vestibule door to my room opening. It is not a nurse because I would hear gowns and gloves being applied, noises that break the silence.

An old gnarled hand appears on the door stanchion, shaking, unsteady. Slowly, slowly the door opens. I lay very still, no noise. I feel nervous, apprehensive. When I see his face, I am silent, transfixed. His eyes are glazed. He seems confused. He looks at me unseeing. The silence is unbroken. He does not speak. His breathing is laboured. I cannot break the silent bond between us. I do not move. He is wearing poorly fitting pyjamas, no slippers, and bare feet. He is lost.

I want to cry; I am not frightened. He does not know I am there. He has crossed the isolation barrier and he does not know I am there; he does not know he is there. We do not share our own silence, our memory, our worlds. So close and yet so far. Two lost souls in isolation.

"Frank, Frank, what are you doing here," says the nurse. She shouts sorry as Frank is led out of isolation and I remain.

I wait for my drinks, meals, medication, observations. Pleasant comments "nice perfume," "cosy room," "how do you feel," "no pain, that's good."

Questions asked are rhetorical, answers not heard, not necessary. The professionals excel in the art of communication where responses are not required. Patients have no faces, no voices, no identity. I am the infection in the cubicle, a clutch of symptoms, an empty vessel, a victim.

Wednesday

My isolation cubicle has a toilet for my exclusive use, a sink, but not an exclusive shower. I feel unclean.

The infection control nurse, gowned and gloved, asks me if I am comfortable. I ask for a shower. A decision is made which will not compromise the other patients and expose them to the isolation patient. If I get up at 6 o'clock before the patients wake, I can go to the shower. I get up and walk through the ward in the dark shadow's unseen. I can see the beds, rooms full of patients. No one can see me. The ward is large. I make it to the shower. My isolation cubicle is at the very end of the ward, the last patient, the last post. I return to my cubicle, back to my routine. But I did get a glimpse of the outside, even if in the shadows, unseen.

I have been in isolation for 9 days. The days and nights have become one. This is now my routine, my life. Am I exaggerating when I say I have become institutionalised? The silence is me; the symptoms are me; isolation is me. I am feeling stronger, my treatment is working. I am sure I will go home soon but I feel ambivalent. Isolation is my life, silence my noise, imagination my friend. I text, talk to my visitors, but I have adapted to my solitude. My fate is in the hands of the professionals.

Thursday

My room is too small. I feel weak but alert. I am better, I am better. The pain is there, or is it better? How do I feel? I want to go home. I do not know what to say. I am so tired, so weak, but does that not mean I am better, just need to build up my strength.

Please do not make me make the decision, I do not know. Please tell me I am better and can go home. Tell me the symptoms have gone, the pain will fade. I do not want to say the wrong thing.

How can I go home, I do not know what to do? I have missed so much. I cannot catch up. I cannot unpack, I cannot do my post, I am too weak. Time has passed. I have been ill for too long. I have missed all this time; I cannot make it up.

Where is everyone, why don't they come, make things alright? I need help; I do not know what to do. I cannot remember home; this is my home. I am frightened. Please tell me what to do, help me.

You told me; I cannot go home. More tests, painful procedures. I cannot go home. I want to cry, to fly, to die. I want to go. I need to stay. Please.

Friday

A restless night, intermittent sleep. I feel Ok this morning, no pain. It is Friday; surely, I will go home before the weekend. I want to go home. I am ready.

The doctor told me the procedures needed would be completed yesterday but that did not happen. The procedures have been arranged for today. They are not pleasant, but I am stronger. I have been nil by mouth for six hours. I am wearing a gown ready to go to theatre. I am alone just waiting. I will have sedation to make me relax. No visitors today because I am having the procedures.

Saturday

I got through the procedures. Drowsy, sore, but in one piece. So much attention from staff in theatre, the doctors. Everything was so fast, so efficient, no talking. Back to isolation, back on my own, back to sleep, silence.

I am stronger, my symptoms are receding, recent memories are beginning to fade, old memories of me are returning. I am aware of my surroundings and I need to go home. I want to go home; I know what to do. I do not belong in isolation; I do not belong anymore. I want to go home.

"Cosy room," "nice perfume," "no pain, that's good," "no bother."

Maria Barrell

Remember Me?

Social Isolation
A disease of the nation
Neighbours no longer look out for each other
Families don't live in with father or mother
So you end up alone
You choose not to leave the family home
Each day the depressing same
       Shame!
Christmas spent in a loveless home
Where only memories make it bearable to be alone
Shared laughter heard in the distance
From those who have forgotten of your existence
People around don't even know your name
       Shame!
So you fight on in your own way
Living your life day after lonely day
Wishing someone would knock on the door
Or a letter would drop to the floor
But you carry on, as it's all you can do
Hoping one day someone will remember you
       Shame!

Tracey Monaghan

Why did I Do That?

Why did I touch my dates tie?
Because the handsome lad caught my eye.
Why did I do that?
Why did I buy a kitten from a pet shop?
When Mam pointed her finger and told me "You Will Not"
Why did I do that?
Why did I throw a dart at a lad at school?
My friend and I thought it was rather cool.
Why did I do that?
Why did I get a curly perm? My hair was long and straight.
It made me look older my hubby did not rate.
Why did I do that?
Why did I make two pies one savoury one sweet?
Serve them on a plate with chips the one without the meat!
Why did I do that?
Why did I walk over Saltwell Parks frozen lake?
Stupid I know, it could have been a big mistake.
Why did I do that?
Collecting grasshoppers down by the Tyne.
Picking up empty coffee cups on the train line.
Why did I do that?
Why did I love Sunday school at Vine Street Mission?
Presented with books from the Sister for my recognition.
Why did I do that?

Mandy Baharie

Ben Swift

Statement of Mary Burrows - Parlour Maid.

My name is Mary Burrows I am a parlour maid employed by Mr Joseph Wilson of Bensham Manor. I am 21 years of age. I first saw Ben on the night of the 21st March, it was raining cats and dogs and little fishes when I heard a loud bang on the back door. Not a little concerned I hurried thence. Whereupon opening the said door I was confronted by a huge man silhouetted against the lightning, "Shit!" said I.

After guiding the shivering giant to the bonny fire which blazed in kitchen grate, I handed the visitor a towel and a tot, then left him with Mrs Redmond the cook, whilst I galloped upstairs to the master's study. After a perfunctory knock the master bade me enter. "There's another big black man at the back-door sir! Much bigger than the last one, built like a brick-sh--!"said I.

"Yes, yes, you need elaborate no further. I have advance warning of his err, prodigious dimensions," the master interjected, as he stroked his beard.

"But where are we to hide him sir? He's too big for the coalhouse," I advised.

"Where is the poor soul now Mary? Have you left the wretch to shiver in the rain?" he replied quite sharply.

Somewhat aggrieved at the master's tone, and the direction of his question, for I am as good a Christian as the next, I answered thus," Why no master, I took him in to the kitchen, sat him next to the fire, then furnished him with a towel, and a nip of the cooking sherry. Also, I doubt not that Mrs Redmond plies him with her very best vittels as we speak!"

"Why, yes of course you would, sorry to have doubted you, poor bairn!" he smiled.

The master stood thinking for a while, "Does the mistress know of our guest yet, Mary?"

"Why, no sir, she is reading in the parlour," I replied.

"Good, good, the dinner guests are not expected for another hour, which with a bit of luck will give us plenty of time and opportunity. Let us make haste child," the master ordered.

The house was silent and still as I guided the visitor down the servant's staircase, the master had ordered that we hide the fugitive in our bedroom whilst the dinner party progressed, but not before the fire was banked and we gave him spare blankets to rest on the floor. It was not easy to carry his blankets and lead him back down the narrow staircase as he shivered so, but never a complaint crossed his lips. The kitchen was lit by a roaring fire as he arranged the blankets and bade him rest. I left a jug of water a next him and made to leave when the man spoke.

"What is your name child?" he asked in tones deep and mellow such as would grace any church or chapel.

Startled I answered thus, "Why my name is Mary, Mary Burrows I am the parlour maid here, but that's just a posh name for a skivvy!"

"Skivvy, what is this skivvy? I have never heard this word before?" he replied in his deep and melodious voice.

" By you American's divvent half tark queer!" I laughed.

"Now you have completely lost me, I understand you not!" he replied with a laugh.

" God bless you sir, skivvy tis but a name for a servant such as I!" I laughed in turn.

The man made to reply but was seized by a paroxysm of shaking such as I had never before beheld. I had taken my shawl and laid it over him, at which point his hand suddenly gripped mine.

"I fear little Mary that Ye may be as much a slave as I," he said.

Perplexed by this strange statement I could only answer, "Why yes, sir, if it pleases you!"

When I returned to the kitchen next morning, he had vanished, phantom like, into the ether.

Statement of William Sherwood.
Vicar of Ladywood, in the Parish of Ravensworth.

I attended Bensham Grove on the 21st March last, for dinner at the behest of my old friend Joseph. Joseph Wilson that is. It was as usual a capital meal, much enriched by the quality of the other guests, the debate of current issues ebbed and flowed across the dinner table like some great storm of intellectual musing.

For myself, I sat on the shore of this tempestuous sea, content to bathe in the reflected considerations of those more knowledgeable on these issues, than I. Late in the hour Joseph somehow manoeuvred the discussion to the subject of slavery in the America's. I cast him a reproachful glance, but he just grinned back slyly.

"Come on William, I am sure you must have something to say on this issue! After all you have been as quiet as a church mouse all night. If you will forgive that dreadful pun gentlemen!" he declared, as the others banged the table in approval.

"Well gentlemen, my view, as you will probably already know, has changed not a jot.

To me slavery is a vile abomination, an evil intolerable to the Christian, in the modern world!" I declared evenly.

"Bravo!" roared Joseph.

"Nonsense! Their economy, for good or ill is dependent on slavery!" Price yelled back.

"That statement is by its very volition self-incriminating! No truly Christian and free society of men, can or should depend on the bonded servitude of others, for its survival!" I declared my right hand held high, like the truly professional orator, I was surely not.

The others blinked back in silence, at this meek church mouse turned lion, as Joseph smiled on approvingly.

I was, I am ashamed to admit it, yawning quite hugely as I made to collect my things.

"Can you spare me a moment young Billy?" Joseph declared, catching my arm.

"Oh, I should have guessed you had something in mind when, I became, somehow or other, the last of your honoured guests to take his leave.

"What is it this time?" I replied wanly.

"Something very close to your heart, my dear boy!" he replied leading me up the back staircase to the servant's quarters.

"Have you taken leave of your senses Joseph what are we about up here?" I remonstrated.

"Nothing that a good Christian would have anything at all to fear, William!" The voice which startled me so, was that of the mistress of the house Mrs Watson. Who dear lady, clapped her hand firmly on my shoulder from behind and guided me most surely in the wake of her husband.

My mind was in a turmoil, how could I possibly explain this bizarre chain of events to Mrs Sherwood? Without the merest shade of hesitation Wilson lead us through the door to apprehend a prone figure shivering under blankets, in a square room rendered tropical by a blazing fire. I stood back in awe as Mrs Wilson laid back the blanket, to reveal a huge black face at once sweating, and next moment frozen into a teeth chattering thrall.

"Poor man!" I declared, bending over him. "What terrible misery has rendered you thus?"

Joseph placed a loving arm, over his now standing wife. "William Sherwood, churchman, be pleased to meet Ben Swift, escaped slave!" he declared through glistening eyes.

I had examined my timepiece for the third time, before Wilson reappeared, his good lady, retiring to bed in order not to arouse suspicion.

"Well, that thank you speech to the servants in the hallway, bought little Mary sufficient time to spirit Ben back a downstairs to the kitchen!" he declared rubbing his hands in conspiratorial glee, as a young boy might in some schoolyard knock about scheme. I could discern that he was indeed, unlike I, enjoying this.

"Nay-Joseph, I cannot in all conscience help you this time. I am a sorry!" I declared firmly, as we sat in the drawing room, our coffee cups lonely on the huge table.

"I truly understand William, is it funds for the roof again?" he enquired.

I smiled back, "Yes, and funds for the poor house, my garden fence, funds for young William's education, Mrs Sherwood's new drapes, new dresses for my girls. Young Ravensworth's back, there is a ball in the offing!"

"Yes, I heard he had returned," Watson replied vacantly. "Of all people I felt wrongly, as it turns out, that I could rely on you William. For as I have related many times you are more of the Christian man, than the Church Man! Bill in conscience, how can you refuse to help or were they just empty words you pronounced at the dinner table?" he continued.

"You, Joseph Wilson are a wicked, sly Quaker Man, but without doubt the most practical Christian person I have ever met. Yes, I will call an early for Ben, and take him in the carriage to Ladywood. Where he can stay in comfortable seclusion, until he be restored in body and spirit. Now Joseph may I ride home? Tis few scant hours till dawn!" I replied feeling tired of body but restored of heart.

Statement of Ben Swift Escaped Slave.

My name for as long as I could remember was Ben, no surname, I was Ben, slaves like animals don't need second names. I escaped when my master took me to a mart in Charleston, being a good servant, he unshackled me, trusting that I would not take my chance at freedom, or the chance of freedom when it came. I did.

The hurricane threw the whole region into chaos, the masters' accommodation collapsed, the walls of my temporary prison having caved in I ran, not looking back, nor returning to rescue my jailer.

I ran for days, the authorities too preoccupied with the hurricane to worry about one runaway slave. I reached the harbour and stowed away on a vessel, not realising that this would be the cause of much further travail. My puny supply of stolen food and water soon dwindled, and I was forced to leave the safety of the hold to forage for the necessities of life.

Fortunately for me the crew were a bunch of rum soaked layabouts, and I was able to garner scraps from their table as they succumbed nightly to the bounty of their liquor.

However, a storm roared up on the third night of my seaborne captivity. Asleep in the hold I was awoken by the scream of the tempest, and the moaning and grinding of the rigging, whilst faint calls of alarm emanated from the deck. Grabbing a loose securing line, I attempted to shelter from the torrent now pouring through the deck covers. Hammered by a huge wave the ship suddenly shuddered and heeled over to port, she had broached and would surely sink. Ignorant of all this I clung onto my line, as in darkness, my world turned upside down, then the hungry turbulent sea blasted into the hold.

I awoke to a raging sea, entangled in the line, but still attached to the huge wooden box from the hold, there was no sign of the crew, nor indeed their vessel. The storm abated at last, and I was able to wriggle free of the line, and clamber exhausted onto the box. I was encouraged in my efforts by the sight of sharks patrolling the debris.

The sun rose pitilessly on the morn, from being soaked and shivering, I was now baked relentlessly by the tropical sun, my only redress, to carefully lap seawater onto my fevered frame, for to thrash carelessly at the surface would be to chance the attentions of the ever alert sharks.

I was thus afflicted for four days and nights, growing steadily weaker, tortured by hunger thirst and sunburn, my only relief, the rain delivered by the occasional squall. On the morn of the fifth day the main flew into another tempestuous rage, huge waves assailed my flimsy ark, and I felt that I was on the crest of that seething wave, betwixt life, and the eternal.

My grip was slipping and as I prepared to make peace with my maker my exhausted mind was transfixed by the words of the 23 psalms.

"The Lord is my shepherd,
I shall not want.
He maketh me lie down in green pastures,
He leadeth me beside the still waters. --"

Then just as suddenly as it came, the storm abated, and as I shaded my eyes from the renewed glare, I could discern in the distance the gleaming upper works of a British Man O' War, and by thus means I was preserved from the oceans' wrath.

I remember nothing of the next five days, as I lay fever ridden, in the sick bay of HMS Swift. The frigate was in urgent passage to London, with the latest intelligence of the Civil War, then raging in my unfortunate country. Before entering the Thames, I was offloaded onto a collier bound for Newcastle.

' To prevent further complications Ben Swift,' the young Lieutenant smiled as he shook my hand. It was the first time that a white man had acknowledged me thus.

I was much improved by this stage, although I must confess that the rough and foggy North Sea, with its biting winds did little to aid my convalescence. Accoutred in a stout naval jacket, scarf, gloves, and mariners' breeches, I still felt the Northern chill as the collier sailed upriver from Tynemouth.

As we journeyed thus, sights assailed my eyes such as formally could only be conjured up in bad dreams. An eerie fog lay low on the river's surface, a topped by layers of thick black smoke which emanated from innumerable factory chimneys. Great bangs and thuds rang out from each riverbank, as huge flares arose from furnaces, the river itself seemed chock full of traffic, making navigation difficult at best. Darkness was falling, to make the gloom complete, when we at last tied up to a quayside, aside a huge city, looming on either bank of the river.

The ague assailed me again, as I said my goodbyes and was helped into a waiting carriage, to the obvious relief of the crew members, and captain. A thunderstorm broke out as we made our way up ill lit, grimy streets, the lightening bringing into occasional focus a thin faced phantom sloshing through the running wet pavements.

In but a few minutes I found myself deposited at the rear entrance of what appeared to be quite a grand house. A young maid answered my knock and stood back in some consternation at my dishevelled appearance, feeling worse by the minute I was led first to a kitchen area, and from thence to the servant's bed chamber.

Sometimes sweating, and at others freezing I lay beneath a blanket in the servants' quarters. However, my miserable solitude was soon broken by a kindly looking man and his lady, they both held lamps and proceeded to question me.

"How are thee poor soul. How may we help ease thy distress?" the man said.

"Really, Joseph isn't it obvious, the man has the ague. We must send for Dr North!" his lady snapped.

"What is thy name poor fellow? Our network which delivered thee to my door, omitted to relate that detail," the man declared.

"My name, sir, is Ben Swift, but I took my second name from the British ship which saved me from the maw of the sea," I wheezed.

"Enough Joseph, let the poor soul rest. You must speak with Mr Sherwood. We must act quickly!" the lady declared.

Sometime later they both returned with another kind faced man, who seemed to be ill at ease in this place, although when he looked over to me his smile was warm and caring, they spoke in hushed tones amongst one another and so I drifted back into the realm of dreams.

I was again disturbed by the servant girl Mary, whose tired worn features, informed me that perhaps a more genteel slavery operated even in this place, but, that nonetheless, slavery it be. The girl led me with difficulty downstairs to the kitchen where I lay under blankets until dawn, when the master of the house and the kind clergyman led me to a carriage.

Mr Sherwood piled more blankets onto me as we set off and gave me a nip of whisky from his hipflask," Fear not Ben Swift I have a feeling that this is the start of a better life for ye!" he declared with a smile.

The birds were singing sweetly, as passing the windmills we progressed down a worn road to a deeply wooded valley, which even had a castle peeping out from the trees.

Travelling on we came to a sleepy little hamlet betwixt the woods, with a tiny church, and an old stone bridge, under which a fresh stream sparkled and murmured, as it meandered along the valley floor. Upon driving over the little bridge, I marvelled at the hoar frost that gilded the gentle downs, aside the river.

I was reminded of how, in the grip of the tempest, on those tumultuous seas, the lord had soothed me with the words of the 23 Psalm, visions of still waters and green pastures. Had I not now indeed found such a place? Sweet tears flowed down my face as I realised that I had at last found my own promised land!

Barry Ross

My Holiday Romance

Her blood red lips, her raven hair, no doubt we make a
handsome pair
And once again, I take the chance, again I begin another
holiday romance
We wine we dine, hand in hand we stroll, on golden sands
under cliffs so tall
Under dappled woods, and by river walk, a different language
but in love we talk

The sun goes down, in rapture we lie, on stack of hay new
bonds we tie
But all too soon, it is time to leave, oh what a tangled web we
weave
To return again, is a promise I make, again we may stroll
beside the blue lake
Again in the straw, in rapture to lie, side by side as the moon
crosses the sky

Money is saved, onto airplane I board, before very long I will
meet my sweet Maud
Our romance to renew, again we do meet, through customs I
pass she is there to greet
Her father has brought her, for she cannot drive, waiting for
hours for me to arrive
My suitcase is packed, in the boot it is placed, and away we
drive at a very slow pace

But the road that we take, leads not to the town, over the hill
and down dale I begin to frown

We stop at the church, there we alight, family and friends have
all gathered, extremely polite

But her brothers all wait, with loaded gun, and neighbours all
eager to see all the fun

Our daughter is brought in, to meet her dad, reminding of last
year and all the love that we had

The marriage takes place, with shotgun in my ribs, with none
of my jokes or corny ad libs

I now am married, to the most wonderful wife, and am leading
a hard but fulfilling life

Now I help out, on the family's large farm, protective of
Sophie shielding her from all harm

My shotgun loaded, for her holiday romance, that's for the
future I will not take that chance

Harry Mason

Just A Boy

Mam, I'm signing up
No you're not lad, yes I am Mam
But you're just a boy
No I'm not Mam, yes you are lad
You're only just seventeen
Yes I know Mam, then why lad
I want to be like my Dad
No you don't lad, yes I do Mam
He went in the army
Yes I know lad, well there you go Mam
But he was killed there
Yes I know Mam, so don't go lad
I want to make you proud
There's no need lad, yes there is Mam
He thought the world of you
Did he Mam, yes he did lad
Well, you're not going to change my mind
Oh, don't go lad, I have to Mam
You're just like your Dad
Am I really Mam, yes you are lad
And you couldn't stop him either
No I couldn't lad, so let me go Mam
It's so hard to see you go
I'll be fine Mam, I hope so lad
Wish me luck then
I do lad, thank you Mam
God bless you son
Goodbye Mam, goodbye lad

Tracey Monaghan

Cinderella

In the back of the Ford Transit, Karam was cold, wet and bloodied. His heartbeat in his throat. Every bump in the road hurt. The gaffer tape binding his wrists and ankles cut into his cold waxen flesh. The gag choked, forcing his breath through his nose. Only able to sit upright until the next corner or when the van braked, he rolled, braced himself.

The van came to a stop. Karam shuffled to the back doors. Lined with plywood, covered in paint and dirty scuffs, the windows were covered in reflective foil. He looked down the length of his body to work out what was causing the pain. His black bomber jacket was pulled up to his shoulders, his fingers and hands covered in scrapes and scuffs, his jeans wet in large patches. He was grass stained and mud spattered. One foot was colder than the other, his right foot shoeless and sockless, throbbing with pain.

Tariq's face was bloodied and wet from tears. He looked over at Karam. Karam shrugged.

In the cab, spindly roll-ups were lit and passed between the occupants of the bench seat. Amidst the tobacco fug, they exchanged congratulations, patted one another on the back.

'Can tell you've been working out…picked him up like a frightened rabbit, that skinny 'un. Clean and jerk. Thought you about to press him up above your shoulders!'

'I'll do it when we get there. Happy to get the guns out.'

'Where now? Should I follow Billy's Golf?'

'Nah. Take the A38. MacDonald's anyone? Calories for when we get there?'

'What about the, erm…cargo?'

No MacDonald's and no full English for them tomorrow morning, I'd be thinking.'

Flashes of blue light illuminated the motorway. The patrol car slowed, pulling onto the hard shoulder.

Beyond the guard rail was a drop, sudden and steep. Raindrops on the grass were picked out in the car headlights.

Reflected light skimmed the wet tarmac. Every nobble and bump in the surface visible. Opening the vehicle door, the officers put on their caps and silently surveyed the scene. Sharp shards of rain furrowed their brows, their eyes narrowed in the darkness.

The police radio on Burden's lapel crackled and spat.

'Charlie-delta-six to base. Exact location of this incident please?' he asked. He looked at his colleague, whose eyes darted around, scouring beyond the guard rail. Plumes of frozen breath unfurled from the officer's nose and lips.

'Incident reported beside emergency phone, ID 767. Four IC1 males handling two IC6 males on hard shoulder. One vehicle nearby, red VW Golf, index November-delta-one-five-golf-Yankee- foxtrot. Believed stolen plates. Running checks on ANPRs in vicinity to locate vehicle. Report when checks made please.'

'Weird.' muttered Malik, warm breath funnelling from the raised collar of his service waterproof. 'We're in the right place. Only one person rang it in? A scuffle at the side of the motorway?' Approaching the guard rail, the officers shone their torches across the grassy drop in front of them.

'No tyre marks. Bit of road rage between boy racers?' speculated Malik. 'God, my stomach is rumbling. Is it buttie o'clock yet?'

'But just the red Golf? For six guys? Must've been a second car, especially the way they're built around here. You and your stomach. Like that plant, Audrey! Feed me now! I don't have a good feel about this. Let's look down this slope. We'll call time if there's nothing else.'

Slicing the soles of his boots into the incline, Burden smiled.

'This is how mountain sheep feel,' he muttered. 'And, by the way, it's your turn at The Greasy Spoon when we're done.'

Malik disappeared, landing with a bump at the bottom of the slope. His grunt echoed through the darkness. Burden smiled, until the cold hurt his teeth.

'Yes, I am OK, thanks mate. Found this. Tripped over it.'

Malik produced a black Puma training shoe. A man's, worn and muddy, its laces still tangled in a tight knot.

'You were right mate. Looks like we've just missed our Cinderella.'

When the engine stopped, the van was in total darkness. Karam could hear the hoot of an owl close-by. Tariq cried beside him. The padlock securing the back doors rattled against the outside as the key was turned. The door-handle creaked, the door opened. Karam squinted out into the darkness.

Moonlight illuminated skeletal trees lining the brow of a distant hill. And the silhouettes of his captors.

Alwyn Bathan

Summer Picnic

For a moment he thought it was snow, the patch of white dazzlingly bright in the sunlight. He laughed at himself for the thought on such a bright July day but, if not snow, what was it?

As he drew nearer, he saw it was a white cloth, a heavy linen cloth, spread out on the grass and weighed down at each corner by four small metal weights each in the shape of an elephant. He didn't know why but he began to smile at the sight of these. There was no one in sight. The river flowed past catching the sun and slightly blinding him. He looked towards the trees growing thickly, about three metres from the river. There was no movement, no sign of anyone. On the riverbank there was only a snowy cloth and four small silver coloured elephants.

He ought, of course, to continue his walk. The cloth had nothing to do with him, but somehow, he needed to know why it was there. He settled down beside a tree in a position to see but not be seen. It was so quiet. There was no breeze. The river rippled and gleamed and the trees cast dark green shadows onto the grass.

The small boy just seemed to be there. When did he arrive? And the white cloth now supported two glasses and a covered jug of pale liquid which was perhaps, lemonade. On folded napkins there were sandwiches and some small cakes under a transparent cover.

The man could not remember when the change had come about. "How strange," he thought. "And the boy? So old fashioned in a Janet and John sort of way."

It was unsettling how the scene changed without his being aware of anything happening. When did the woman arrive? When did she and the boy begin their picnic, chatting and laughing together?

He felt lightheaded. "The sun on the river," he thought. "It's making me dizzy."

He was suddenly aware: suddenly apprehensive. He felt his heart thudding in his chest, and he knew without any doubt what would happen next.

The woman would lie back in the warm sunshine and despite herself, her eyes would close for a few seconds. The boy would wander to the river's edge declaring his intention to give one of the little elephants a drink and he would tumble in.

The man knew. He knew for certain as once again he fought the river in blind panic. As once again he called for his mother. As once again the water closed above him and the undercurrent carried him away.

Maureen C Bell

Doorways

She is alone, unloved, forgotten and ignored
Passers-by blind to her sadness and desperation
Simply go about their business and cross the road
The cold hard stone she sits on penetrates her frail body
Through the rags she wears once which were her clothes
What she would give for a warm coat and hot toddy!

To ease the pain and suffering she has her dreams
And sees herself happy and loved in a good home
Children and music playing, but not is all as it seems
This is her and her sister separated when so young
Only in her mind can she see her now
In a family and having fun

No one came for her at the institution
She had never felt wanted and really loved
But running away from this had not been the solution
London was not paved with gold as she had heard
She had seen people like her lonely and in need

Someone should have spread the word

After years of living this homeless life
A kind person couldn't entice her to a home
It was a shelter run by himself he said and his wife
The changing seasons bring their challenges
Too hot, too cold, too wet
But proof of her here today tells me she still manages

This could happen to anyone of us and at any time
A job loss, a breakup, mental illness or too much debt
We could be that person in the soup kitchen waiting in line
Life can give you really good and bad days
But there is always home, laughter and music in between
We need to cherish what we have or we could end up in that
doorway!

Tracey |Monaghan

I Love You

I love rising early on a summer's day
I like the end of the week when I get to play
I like a pint at my local pub
I like a biscuit, a penguin of an orange club
I like eating a Scone and a hot big Casserole
A game of football, when I score a goal

I like a stroll through fields of pretty flowers
A walk in the park especially at Saltwell Towers
I love to love a lovely pretty girl
Her lovely face and hair send me into a whirl
I love to lounge on a lovely soft pink cushion
A big hot apple pie that gets me all gushing

Tom Gallagher

Shake it Baby

It's time to waltz away weekday blues
To don, the patent leather shoes
To glide across the wooden base
In rhyme and beat and full of grace
To tango to a trendy song
Two forms as one, absorb the throng

Sweet music from the ballroom band
We'll jive away with hand in hand
We'll rock and roll and twist and shout
And flout our forms and let it out
We'll quickstep to a tricky tune
We'll listen to the singer croon

We'll dance and dance the night away
Our bodies heave with sweat and sway
It's time to kiss and say goodbye
These precious times oh how they fly

Tom Gallagher

The Doorway to Hell

It was a chilly autumn morning I was busy getting ready to meet my friend Stacey. We met up once a week for either a shopping trip, lunch or a walk in the park. Nothing is rarely planned just one of us will text to see if we fancied doing whatever? I was just finishing breakfast when I read her message. 'Morning do you fancy a trip to Durham?'

'Yes,' I replied back to her. 'Great meet at the bus stop 10 o'clock, don't be late' she texts back.

An hour later we were sitting chatting in a warm cosy coffee shop drinking frothy lattes. When we had finished, we zipped up our coats and headed for the door.

"Excuse me ladies" a woman's voice said. As we turned to see who was talking to us, I noticed that the coffee shop had emptied we we're all alone. The autumn sun was very bright, as it shone through the window, we could see the old lady standing in the doorway behind us. The light illuminating her grey wiry hair. Her face looked translucent against the shadows, beady eyes watching us. Our eyes were drawn to her bright red lipstick, and I noticed her lips were twitching nervously.

"Can you use the back door?" she said as she pointed a bony finger behind her.

"You see I've just washed the floor I wouldn't want you to slip," she smiled showing lipstick stained yellow teeth.

"Oh, sorry yes of course," Stacey said.

"Can we get down to the river that way," I asked. "We fancy a nice walk."

"Oh yes," she said slowly nodding her head. "Just follow the path along the alley."

She held a red velvet curtain open to let us through. The back of the shop was dimly lit, and the faded peeling wallpaper was coming away from the walls. The carpet stained and worn was disgusting.

"Oh God hurry up let's get out of here," I said wrinkling my nose. "Where the hell are we Becky," Stacey said with a nervous laugh.

"I don't know but hurry up I need some fresh air."

We edged our way a little further then noticed two doorways.

"Which one? Stacey said as she stared at the doors in front of her.

"Just try one," I said.

"One's got to be a cupboard," Stacey pointed out as she took hold of the round black handle, but it was locked.

She tried the handle on the next door, we heard a click and the door squeaked open. A musty smell filled our nostrils. Once our eyes had adjusted to the light, we saw a narrow pathway covered with coloured leaves ahead of us. Dry stone walls on either side covered with ivy and bracken.

"Where are we," Stacey said as she looked along the path.

"I've no idea, but let's get away from here. She scared the hell out of me in there."

Stacey agreed. "She was creepy, I didn't notice her."

Me neither, I thought. We hurried along the pathway in single file.

"This looks like a dead end."

"It can't be," I said as I pushed past her.

Stacey was right, a wall blocked us going any further. Ivy clung to every crevasse.

"I can't believe this," Stacey said shaking her head. "We'll have to go back to the coffee shop," I replied.

Stacey starred at the ivy clad wall. "What's that?" she said looking closely. "Becky is that a door handle?"

"Where," I said frowning.

"Here look," she said pulling ivy away from the wall.

Suddenly I saw a worn ornate rusty handle. "You're right," I said as I helped her pull long clinging tendrils away. "There's a doorway, oh, it's covered in cobwebs," I cried.

"Never mind that, let's just hope it opens," she said as she pushed down hard on the handle. The door moved a couple of inches then got stuck.

"Let's turn around and go back to that shop. I'm not going in there it looks filthy," I said. Thankfully Stacey agreed.

We heard the fierce growl before we had a chance to turn around frozen to the spot, I managed to look over my shoulder. Standing behind us was a huge vicious black dog, snarling and barring its teeth.

"Stacey, when I tell you," I said slowly. "Push that door with all your might."

Stacey nodded and closed her eyes. I could sense the dog getting closer. "Now!" I shouted. We both kicked and pushed the jammed door. It swung open to reveal steep slippery steps.... There was silence, I turned around the dog had disappeared.

"What's that smell Becky?"

"I think it's sulphur," I said. It seemed to be a mixture of that and rotten leaves, I thought.

"It stinks," Stacey exclaimed. "What now Becky?"

"We'll have to go down there," I said as I looked into the darkness.

Stacey's frightened face stared at me "We can't Becky, we'll break our necks. There's nothing to hold on to?"

She was right the steps had no supporting wall or handrail.

"Stacey, that dog could come back and attack us any time soon, I'm scared too?"

She let out a sigh and took hold of my hand. "Come on then just be very careful."

Gingerly we made our way further into the darkness. A flicker of light in the distance gave us both a fright. "Did you see that?" I said.

Stacey nodded. Then the chanting. Terror ran through my veins, "Did you hear that?" I whispered.

Stacey didn't say anything she just squeezed my hand tightly. Further down we went eventually our feet trod on rotten wet leaves. The flicker of light was getting brighter, and the chanting was getting louder.

"I can see people," Stacey exclaimed.

Straining my eyes to see, I could see hooded figures. "Oh my God, Stacey, they're monks!" We were terrified, where were we? The chanting grew louder, and we could see the procession more clearly.

"I can make out six," Stacey whispered in a shaky voice.

I could see they were holding long white candles. Their thick brown robes trailing the sodden ground. Suddenly one of them turned and looked in our direction. We gasped and held our breath. Stacey panicked and let out a scream! The monk had no face, only blackness filled it's hood. Terror gripped me, but I managed to grab Stacey by the arm. We ran as fast as we could stumbling over gnarled tree roots.

"Becky I can't run anymore. Leave me here you go and get help," she pleaded.

I looked around me and could see the flickering candles coming nearer! Looking straight ahead straining my eye's in the darkness. I thought my mind was playing tricks on me I thought I saw a stream of light in the distance. I blinked and rubbed my eyes. The light was definitely there! Gradually it dawned on me the light was coming from a doorway.

"Get up Stacey," I screamed. "I can see a door!"

The chanting stopped, holding our breathes and slowly turning around we saw six faceless figures standing in a line behind us.

"Stacey run for your life, run towards the light" I screamed. Reaching the door, I flung it open and we ran right through it.

I woke myself up just as I was about to hit the ground. Confused and shaking it suddenly dawned on me it had all been a terrifying nightmare!

My mind replayed the whole thing over and over it felt so real.
Eventually I drifted back off to sleep. My mobile phone woke
me up later that morning, a text I thought. Picking up my phone
I read the message from Stacey. Morning, do you fancy a trip to
Durham today?

Mandy Baharie

Stay Here Awhile My Love

I know you will be angry, that I did not go out today
I could not face the world outside; I have nothing I want to say
You told me to carry on, to live my normal life
Be brave and show the world, I am your strong loving wife

I cannot pretend to be a wife, without my husband by my side
You said I had an inner strength, but it was only for you I tried
Loneliness surrounds me; it reaches down into my soul
The darkness is all encompassing, as I fall into the hole

I want to be with you, my life has no meaning now
There are no family around me, no friends to show me how
How to adjust to loneliness, to learn to live again
All I have are your memories; they help to ease my pain

I talk to you every day; I imagine what you would say
I know you will be worried, as I waste each precious day
I promised I would make you proud, and hold my head up high
But I am so lonely now; I do not want to try

At night I remember, how close we could entwine
I sleep alone with your memory, for your touch I always pine
I really miss your snoring, although I did complain
I cannot deal with the silence; it is driving me insane

It has been over a year now, since your heart stopped, and you
died
You were so ill but came home, and together we laughed and
cried
We were in each other's arms, when I felt you slip away
I knew you had left me; there was nothing else to say

Stay here a while my love, and help me one more time
I need you to be proud of me, to know I am doing fine
I will try very hard my love, to make my life worthwhile
To show I am your loving wife, I will try to make you smile

Maria Barrell

The Locket in the Charity Shop

Annette tidied the bric-a-brac shelf repositioning the vases, worn leather purses, odd candle sticks and straightened the books.

"Don't forget to sweep the floor tonight," called Phyllis, the manageress.

Annette ground her back teeth knowing in the six weeks she'd worked there she'd never once forgotten to sweep the shop floor. Phyllis reminded her of an old headmistress she'd worked for years ago at the secondary school. Full of her own importance but at the same time Annette could tell she lacked in self-confidence.

Brushing into the corner of the window she sighed. The display looked dreadful. It was a mismatch of old clothing and shoes which had been there for months. There was nothing to appeal to passers-by or entice customers inside. She tutted, just because it was a small shop outside Durham this didn't mean it couldn't look as good as the well-known Oxfam shop in the city.

Annette pulled on her denim jacket with a torrent of ideas whizzing through her mind about dressing the window, if given the chance. She unlocked her bicycle and cycled home knowing exactly what items she'd pair together for the window.

With a cup of tea, she waited for her daughter, Emma, to skype from Australia. Emma had emigrated five years ago, and Annette still missed her even though they were in regular contact and visited as often as they could.

She remembered Emma's reaction when she'd told her about her new job.

"You're going to work in a charity shop!"

"Er, yeah, there's nothing wrong with charity shops," she'd said. "You know I've always loved a good rummage?"

Emma had sighed. "But, Mum, you're supposed to be retired and looking after yourself!"

She'd seen the wariness in her daughters' big blue eyes on the screen and didn't want her to worry. "And, I am looking after myself, darling, but I'm only sixty-three and I need something to do with my days. I need structure. I can't busy myself with housework and coffee mornings?"

"Okay, Mum, but you know the doctor said it was because of the stressful workload of teaching that had caused the panic attacks?"

She'd smiled. "No, Emma, he said, it had contributed to my poor mental health, and that stressful situations can trigger the attacks. But I've told you how I manage the panic attacks now which are very few and far between."

They'd agreed that as it was only three days a week, she'd see how it went for a few months. However, so far, she was really enjoying mixing with the other volunteers and loved helping the customers with their purchases. They were a mix of students, middle-aged, and old people, and sometimes a few homeless people who drifted inside. In her mind, she thought of the work as giving something back to the community, and the sense of well-being at the end of the day had amazed her.

***

The next morning, she began to open four black sacks of donations that had arrived into the storeroom. One sack was full of dresses which sent her into a tizzy. She'd always loved fashion and because her mother had been a dressmaker, she'd inherited her appreciation of good quality fabrics, style and the cut of a decent cloth. She smiled remembering her mother's favourite saying, "There's nothing like the feel of pure silk between your fingers."

Annette pulled a navy-blue polka dot dress from the sack and grinned. It looked like something Audrey Hepburn would have worn.

She remembered a similar dress she'd had but in cream and brown dots. Her ex-husband, John, had said, "That dress is perfect on you, it really matches your eyes."

He'd given her a wolf-whistle which at the time had made her feel special, but now she shrugged her shoulders with indifference. John had been a CEO of a huge business and travelled all over the world during the years they were married. But seven years ago, he somehow forgot to come home and moved-in with a younger model in Milan.

Shrugging his memory from her mind Annette delved deeper into the sack and put the dresses onto size 12 clothes-hangers on a rail. There were two beautiful ball gowns in pink chiffon and a green taffeta. A slight whiff of perfume filled the air, Coty L'aimant, she wondered, of one of the original Channel perfumes? Whichever it had been, Annette knew it was expensive.

Betty popped her head into the doorway. "Annette, Phyllis is going to be off sick this week, so you'll have to cover on the till," she said then sidled over to her. At nearly seventy-five, Betty was the oldest volunteer in the shop and had worked there for years. Slightly eccentric but with the biggest heart one could imagine, Annette loved her honest, down-to-earth attitude.

The old woman took a slow deep breath in awe and touched the array of dresses. "Gosh, these must have cost a pretty packet in their day?"

Anette grinned. "Absolutely. They're beautifully made to measure. There's been none of the, on-the-shelf dresses, for this lady," she said. "I wonder who she was?"

"Hm, I could never afford to buy anything like that when I was younger, being a miner's wife, I was lucky to have enough money to feed the five of us, never mind, expensive clothes."

Annette could tell Betty had slipped back to thoughts of her younger days and she stroked her shoulder.

While emptying the other sack Annette placed two beaded evening purses, a pair of elegant long-sleeved gloves, and an empty jewellery box into the appropriate sections. All the while she kept glancing at the dresses with ideas buzzing around in her mind. She often wished they knew where the donations came from and the background stories that only the clothes could tell.

When Betty left at lunch time Annette began to serve customers at the till as a steady stream of people filled the shop. Annette was folding tissue paper under the counter when someone approached. She looked up to see Sheila Jackson holding two black bags.

Although Sheila wasn't a friend, and lived at the opposite edge of the village, she knew her, like every other villager did because of her tragic circumstances. Sheila's only daughter had been killed in May 2017 at the Manchester Arena terrorist bombing. It had rocked the whole village for months.

Annette smiled. "Hey, Sheila, how are you?" As the words left her mouth, she realised how ridiculous they must sound. "I mean, well…"

"It's okay, Mrs Wilson," she murmured. "No one ever knows what to say."

Sheila lifted one of the bags onto the counter. "I just thought it was time. Well, if there's ever a time to part with her things, it's now. I didn't think I'd ever be able to give her stuff away but I'm trying to clear out and downsize into a small flat. I wondered if they'd be any good for the charity?"

Annette thought quickly. It must be nearly two years now since the bombing and she saw tears moisten Sheila's eyes. "Of course, everything we get is always a great help," she said. "And, Sheila, my name is Annette."

Sheila tilted her head to one side. "Oh, we always knew you as Mrs Wilson from school because you tried to teach my girl maths," she chortled. "We had many sleepless nights with algebra homework which had to be submitted on time!"

Annette remembered her daughter had being in Emma's year at school. "Oh, dear, I hope I wasn't too much of a dragon?"

She shook her grey curly hair and smiled. "Not at all. I knew it was because you wanted all the girls to do well and get good grades in their exams."

Annette remembered Sheila's daughter had gone to college and worked in accountancy, although never marrying, she worked tirelessly at the village community centre. She'd taken a group of teenagers to the Manchester concert, and thankfully, they were all spared because they'd been in another part of the arena when the bomb exploded.

Annette nodded and smiled back at Sheila then lifted the sack up from the floor. It wasn't tied tightly, and Sheila fingered some black lace that was peeking out of the top.

"That was her prom dress," she said wistfully. "I told her at the time black wasn't the best colour to wear, but she insisted."

Annette gasped. She'd forgotten it was that time of year. The summer weeks of giddiness before the all-important annual prom night. She remembered Emma in her silvery long dress shimmering in the hallway waiting for the taxi to arrive.

She swallowed a huge lump in her throat at this other woman's misery. "Oh, God," she muttered.

Sheila hurried to the doorway, as a man approached the till. Annette dropped the bag on the floor and asked the man to wait while she rushed out after her. "Sheila! Wait a minute," she called, but Sheila was way down the street.

By four in the afternoon the shop was empty, and Annette wandered over to the window. It's now, or never, she thought smiling at her plan. As Phyllis wasn't in the shop, she reckoned there was nothing to stop her and giggled with excitement.

She pulled back the drab curtain from the window recess and donned her rubber gloves. Her nose filled with a musty smell from the old clothes and moth balls.

She cleared everything out into a black sack. 'Rubbish bin for them,' she muttered. With a bowl of warm soapy water, she cleaned the whole window then set to work.

There were two old mannequins in the storeroom covered with a sheet and she blew the dust from them. Laughing to herself she now washed the female mannequins. 'You're getting ready for the prom, my girls,' she tittered then carried them into the window.

Annette found pink and silver tissue paper to line the window recess and scattered a box of silver stars over it. She gathered up the evening bags, and found three pairs of high-heeled shoes in silver black and red. She placed these at the bottom of the mannequin's feet and put the pink ball gown on one of the mannequins pinning the back to make it fit. Pulling the long white evening gloves onto the mannequin's arms was a bit of a struggle but she managed and stood back in awe. She looked stunning. This would be how the owner of the dress had looked back in her day.

She dragged a small clothes rail into the recess and hung the other dresses up facing the glass window. Rummaging in the jewellery stand she found a long string of imitation pearls and two gold-plated chains and draped them around the mannequin's necks.

Carefully, she lifted the black lace dress from Sheila's sack to hang on the other mannequin. As she smoothed down the lace, she found a pocket in the side of the dress with something hard inside it?

'What the,' she muttered and pulled from the pocket a silver locket on a chain. Realising Sheila's daughter must have worn this on the prom night, she sighed. Did Sheila know the locket was in the dress? Surely, not, she thought.

A shiver ran down her spine knowing she'd never give anything as precious as this away if it was Emma's? Annette tucked it inside the pocket of her jeans and decided to take it to Sheila the next day.

***

The first sight of the window the next morning made Annette gasp out loud at her own handiwork: the transformation looked amazing. She pulled her mobile from her back pocket and took a quick photograph to send to Emma later. Gingerly, she opened the shop door, and heard Betty pottering about in the storeroom.

"Morning," she called walking through and taking off her jacket.

"Well, now," Betty grinned showing the gaps in her teeth. "I think we've had fairies here during the night doing up the window display?"

Annette giggled. "I couldn't help myself. It looked so drab and we have such great things inside the shop that nobody ever sees," she said. "But Phyllis will go mad, won't she?"

Betty laughed out loud and licked her eccentric bright red lipstick. "Probably, but I'd pay money to see the look on her face when she sees it!"

They both laughed while Betty made tea and Annette explained about the display and how she'd created it to look like prom night. The buzz in the shop lasted all day. Everyone that came inside raved about the dresses and the window display. It took both herself and Betty to serve on the till because they were so busy and by late afternoon, the days takings shot up by 60%.

"So, Annette, that window has certainly done the trick and livened up the place," Betty said getting ready to leave. "And, Phyllis won't be complaining when she sees how much money we've taken. As my old mum used to say, the proof is in the pudding!"

Annette nodded as she noticed a girl and her mum enter the shop. She could tell by their appearance that they were one of the new displaced families in the area that she'd read about in the local newspaper.

Her heart warmed to them. "Can I help? Is there anything you're looking for?"

The girl looked about sixteen with a small pixie face who stared at Annette from under a heavy dark fringe. She looked a little like Emma did at her age and Annette remembered how she'd often bit her lip in awkward situations.

Annette smiled reassuringly at the mother then noticed the girl staring at the dresses in the window. "Would you like to try a dress on?"

Annette reached inside the window to the pink ball gown, but the girl shook her head and pointed to the black lace. She lifted the dress from the mannequin and handed it to her.

The grin on the girl's face reached from one ear to another. "Thank you very much."

Annette wanted to reach out to them and knowing language might be a barrier she put an arm along her shoulder and walked them into the storeroom. The shop wasn't big enough for a changing room, but she really wanted the girl to try the dress on, and because Phyllis wasn't there, for once, it wouldn't matter. Annette left them and hovered outside the door while she changed. She'd heard that the new families were at the secondary school and Annette wondered if the girl was going to the prom?

After a few minutes, she popped her head around the door and gasped. "Gosh, you look absolutely beautiful!"

The girl grinned. "It is good fit, yeah?"

Annette saw tears well up in her mother's eyes. She hurried back to the display and picked up the black shoes, evening bag and the set of imitation pearls. She gave them to the girl who pushed her feet into the shoes.

"They look a little tight?"

But the girl nodded enthusiastically. "No, no, they are okay."

Annette smiled. She supposed after all they'd been through, tight-fitting shoes figured low on their list of priorities. The mother nodded and pulled a small purse from her brown coat pocket. Annette knew the dress was £15 and all in all the whole outfit would come to £20.

The mother pulled out some notes and raised an eyebrow while the girl spoke for her. "How many pounds will that be, please?"

Annette sighed. It didn't matter where in the world you were and what ever circumstances you faced, all that mothers wanted to do was give their daughters something special. She reached over and took a £5 note from the mother.

The girl turned the tag over, looked at the price and furrowed her eyebrows. "Is this correct?"

Annette knew she'd figured the price wasn't right, but she nodded and smiled at her, then handed them a carrier bag and left her to change.

She knew if Phyllis found out she'd be furious, but she didn't care. She opened her own purse and put the other £15 into the till knowing it was worth every penny to give the girl a prom night she'd never forget.

***

Annette walked along the street remembering Sheila Jackson lived in the last terraced house. Vaguely, in the back of her mind she could recall years ago collecting Emma from a sleep-over. She'd tried to work out exactly what she was going to say to Sheila but now she was here, she licked her dry lips.

Sheila opened the door and smiled. She made coffee and they sat together while Annette explained about the pocket in the dress and handed Sheila the locket.

"Oh, thank you so much," Sheila said. "I'd forgotten about the locket. My mother gave it to her for the prom."

Annette smiled. "I thought you wouldn't know it was in the pocket, so I figured, I'd offer it back to you rather than just put it up for sale in the shop?"

Sheila nodded. "That's kind of you, Annette, thanks again."

Annette sipped her coffee and explained about the drab window and how she'd revamped the display into a prom theme with all the other dresses they had. "So, I hoped you wouldn't mind but I put the black lace dress in there?"

Annette pulled out her mobile, scrolled through and showed the photo to Sheila.

Sheila gasped and her whole face lit up. "It looks so beautiful on the model," she said. Annette knew she was remembering her daughter in the dress. She leaned forward and took a deep breath then described the girl and mother who had come into the shop.

Sheila nodded. "Oh, my friend told me some of the families go into the community centre and they've bought stuff at the last jumble sale to furnish their homes."

Annette sighed. "It's so sad, Sheila, they have nothing?"

"I know." Sheila nodded twirling the locket between her fingers. "And my daughter did do all she could to help under-privileged families at the centre."

Annette smiled. "Well, the mother bought the dress for her girl to go to the prom and I gave her the shoes and accessories to match. I think your daughter would have liked to see, that even now, her dress is still helping another girl have a great prom night?"

Sheila clapped her hands together and burst into tears, but Annette knew they were happy tears. "Oh, yes, she would have done! Thank you so much, Annette, she would have loved that!"

Annette took Sheila's hands in hers and squeezed them tightly.

Susan Willis

What Is An Unusual Experience?
What is an unusual experience
Something out of the ordinary
Strange to you
Sometimes a shock
Coming out of the blue
Or could it be a pleasure
Discovering new things
Unearthing some hidden treasure
Of gold and diamond rings
A different experience
The day you rode the 'Big One'
which previously had frightened you to death
That left you feeing exhilarated
And only slightly out of breath
A journey beyond the stars
To galaxies unknown
Flying as a spaceman
Many miles from home
Encountering a ghostly presence
To test your imagination
Giving you a very odd and eerie sensation
Experiences through life can be good or bad
But some can be the most unusual you've ever had!

Tracey Monaghan

Clocks

Doesn't time fly? Tick tock, tick tock. Can you imagine before the invention of the clock? Things must have been quite chaotic.

At work when you look at the clock too frequently time seems to drag. However, if you're doing something pleasant or interesting time does fly.

There's something soothing and relaxing when I hear the chimes of a clock. A certain conformity, it gives us a direction, that we must adhere to.

Those tiny little watches that women wear on their wrists, how the hell do they make those minute working sprockets and wheels?

These time makers must be extremely skilled at measuring and making time pieces.

Tom Gallagher

The Scourge of Plastic

It is in the sea and on the ground
This dreadful stuff is all around
Let's, start to clean, lets, make a start
Yes, everyone will play a part

Plastic here and plastic there
For our children's sake it's time to care
It clogs the guts of all sea creature
It is on the news with disturbing features

Debris here and Debris there
It's all around no time for despair
Cotton buds and baby wipes
Clogs up streams and clogs up pipes

Containers big, cartons just small
We will collect, we will recall
The clean-up army is on the move
In five years', time, it will improve.

Tom Gallagher

Black Magic

Well, there was a black magic woman who had a sweet tooth.
Tall dark and mysterious, she was over six foot.
She lived deep in the forest all by herself.
Potions and spell books on every shelf.
Her passion was dark chocolate from the cocoa tree.
She made pretty boxes tasty and free.
Then cast up a spell to make them taste good.
In a state of ecstasy, they lightened her mood.
But one day in the forest a man found her stash.
Licking his lips, he said "I'll have some of that"
Black magic woman cursed and she swore.
Never in her life had this happened before.
Out in the forest she started to dance.
Chanting and shaking she went into a trance.
The whites of her eyes rolled into her head.
Voodoo took hold as if she were dead!
"Whoever eats my chocolates" she cursed.
"Will have fatal consequences and come of worse"
The man now far away, sat down on a log.
Popped a chocolate in his mouth and chewed on a poison
frog!!

Mandy Baharie

The Hole in One

It was the biggest day of the year at Robinswell Golf Club. The day had dawned bright and clear, not a cloud in the sky. The forecast was excellent, plenty of sun and a pleasant cooling breeze.

Harry had been waiting for this day, since he had decided to sponsor one of the holes. All the sponsors were allowed to play in this championship, irrespective of their handicap. Harry, with this intention in mind, had finally realised this was the only way he could take part in this prestigious event at his 'second home'. As sponsor of the first hole, it would be his honour to open the championship with the first drive off the opening tee.

Now the big day had arrived, Harry was starting to feel the pressure of his responsibility. He would be playing with Tom James, the current club champion, handicap, scratch, and the club president, Bill Thompson, handicap, one. Harry had a handicap of twenty but had rarely played anywhere near that.

As he stood on that first tee, his nerves were at breaking point. There were a good number of his fellow competitors waiting to follow the opening group, all with handicaps of five or less. He exchanged scorecards with his partners, bent to press his tee into the yielding turf, placed his ball on the tee and said, 'Callaway' number three. His partners both wished him good luck. Now was his moment of glory.

Or that was what passed through his mind as he topped his drive fifty yards down the first hole. He had not even reached the fairway, but it was in the middle, he consoled himself. Bad luck, his partners commented, as they both sent their drives two hundred and fifty yards off the tee. Harry walked up to his ball, took out his trusty rescue club and pulled his second shot into the pond.

Putting a new ball down he informed his partners, 'playing four'. This shot was better, it nearly reached his partners. 'Playing five,' he somehow managed to get his ball onto the green. Well played, his partners commented. Were they really congratulating him, or were they just being sarcastic, Harry thought? Two putts for a seven, he could have done worse, Harry thought to himself. Tom was up and down for three, Bill two putted for par. On to hole two, a par five.

Again, Tom and Bill were in the middle, Tom just bettering Bill by about fifteen yards. Harry stepped up to the tee, and for him, hit a 'cracker,' right down the middle, about one hundred and eighty yards. Well played, his partners commented as they all started off down the fairway. Coming off the second green, Tom again had a birdie, Bill a par, and Harry a creditable seven.

Now to hole three, 390 yards with a massive 'dogleg to the right. It was out of bounds down that right boundary. Tom stepped up and hit a massive drive, cutting across the dogleg and ending about sixty yards from the green. Bill played safe hitting his drive into the neck of the dogleg, a hundred yards short of the green. Harry, now settling down, sliced his drive out of bounds on that right boundary. His next shot followed the first and he was five off the tee. Tom missed the green with his short approach, ending in a bunker. Bill was up and down for three. Tom ending up with a bogey five. Harry just evaded double figures with a nine.

And so, the game progressed. Tom and Bill neck and neck all the way through the sixteenth. Tom holding a single shot lead at this point, four under par. It was safe to say that Harry, at this same point was not in contention. Still, if he could hold things together, he might be able to stay under 120.

It was Tom's honour and he hit a lovely shot, hitting the par three green, and spinning back to about twelve feet from the pin.

Bill stepped up and hit a similar shot, finishing twenty feet away. In such exalted company, Harry was by now, rueing his decision to take part in this championship.

Tom and Bill however, whilst fighting tooth and nail against each other, were both very encouraging to Harry. Not once did they indicate any annoyance at his ineptitude. They were perfect gentleman, offering advice and praising his few good shots.

Harry now came onto the tee. He informed his partners that he was changing his ball again, another 'Callaway' number three. This was his last ball of the box of twelve his wife had bought him for their silver wedding celebrations.

Kissing the ball, he placed it on the tee, stepped back, took a couple of practise swings, then stepped up to the ball and took up his stance. Crack, the ball was away, sliced way off course to the right. His heart skipped a beat and under his breath a curse was forming on his lips when, the ball hit a boundary fence, looped high into the air and disappeared. The expletives issuing from his lips would embarrass anyone.

Play a provisional, his partners advised. Harry's interest in the game was quickly dissipating. He searched in his bag and brought out an old, 'Pinnacle', a little grubby but sound. He again teed off and finished in the greenside bunker on the left.

All three progressed down and through the valley and started searching for Harry's first ball. Five minutes and it was time to play on. Bill and Tom both went onto the green to mark their balls, whilst Harry surveyed his lie in the bunker. Tom was passing the flag and noticed a ball lying snuggly in the hole. Calling the attention of his playing partners to this fact, he bent to retrieve it.

'Callaway number three,' he said, as he stood up. 'Is this yours,' he asked Harry as he handed it over. Harry took the ball and examined it closely, not believing his luck. Tom and Bill both flung their arms around him. A hole in one they were saying. Harry was speechless.

If you knew Harry, you would know that this is not a common occurrence with him. It finally sank in and by this time people on the tee behind were able to see the jubilation on the green in front of them. Tom and Bill putted out, Tom making par and Bill holding out for a birdie, to level their private match.

Now they are onto the final tee. For only the second time since that opening drive, Harry has the honour and sends a booming drive, over two hundred yards down the middle of the fairway. Tom sends his, well offline to the left, and Bill draws level with Harry. Tom is unable to reach the green in two and Bill's second goes into a greenside bunker. Can Harry keep his head and green his second? Yes, it is rolling up the green and is close, giving himself a tap in for birdie. Tom and Bill both make par and tie their private match. Harry is ecstatic. He cannot believe he has holed in one and parred the last two holes.

A round of drinks in the bar, then Harry returns home, to regale his wife with that beautiful bounce he received on the seventeenth and the wonderful chip dead on the last.

Harry Mason

Harvest Moon

A myriad of colours met my eyes as I entered in that day
I gazed in awe and wonder at the abundant display
Of shiny apples, oranges, grapes and more
Along with green vegetables, carrots, parsnips so raw
And taking centre stage was the biggest bread there had ever
been
Fashioned into plaits and sheaves of corn to compliment the
scene
I held my basket made up of favourite fruits but no veg
Carefully fashioned with green crepe around the edge
The container an old mushroom box begged from the shop
All secured tightly in cellophane with silver handle on the top
Proudly with others I carried my gift to the front of the chapel
To have it laid amongst the harvest food next to the shiny
apples
The organ then struck up with a favourite harvest hymn
Of ploughing the fields and seed scattering

It was a sunny morning and all was good in the world
As the chapel soared with music and the festival unfurled

Tracey Monaghan

Trees

Standing tall and proud
Heads above the waving crowd
Stretching out over the scene
Emblazoned with leaves of green
Gentle giant of fragile wood
Some for hundreds of years have stood
Giving food, shelter, succour and shade
Changing seasons see colours fade
Bitter winds leave branches bare
Shrouded in white from winter air
Eerily silhouetted against the night
Shadows thrown in daylight
Secrets of nature to the nations
Trees evolving for future generations

Tracey Monaghan

The Beach

The sky-blue sea so calm and clear,
The pale white sand we love so dear,
The gentle surf laps at our feet,
The constant waves our feet do meet,

We'll walk for miles along the shore,
A distant wave a distant roar,
Sailing boats and distant ships,
That lovely smell of fish and chips,

We're weary now and need some grub,
Just two miles more then it's the pub,
But first we'll relish this lovely day,
We're at South Shields and not Whitley Bay

Tom Gallagher

Harvest

Those large golden fields that dazzle one's eye
Barley and oats, wheat and rye
Combines ready, to move to and fro
A huge big tool, to cut and to mow
Fair weather's here, but not for long
I hear a Linnet, a familiar song

It's time to thresh, make good the day
Trucks full of grain and large spools of hay
This special grass, because it's what they are,
Cover distant hills, so near and far
This precious food will nourish and feed
Its Millers work now to grind the fine seed
The golden crust is what ovens will bake
This tasty fresh food, this crucial make

Tom Gallagher

A Winter's Tale

Now just a memory those hot sultry days
When we enjoyed warm sunshine and outside play
Creeping in slowly colder times ahead
As autumn changes landscapes and flowerbeds
Stripped of their colours trees are stark and bare
A contrast to their summer foliage no longer there
As clocks turn back the nights draw in
Bright days turn to dark mornings
Across paths and grass frosty fingers spread
Windows stream as you get out of bed
Grey skies hold unshed snows
Breath chills in the cold air exposed
Cotton clothes and sun hats all put away
Woollen scarves and hats now the order of the day
Everyone now bracing for whatever winter brings
Looking forward to a warmer spring

Tracey Monaghan

The Jigsaw

Hundreds of pieces concealed in a box
the puzzle to put together its secret to unlock
A fun way to while away some leisurely hours
creating country scenes, animals or garden flowers
Starting with the edges to get the size perspective
working to the middle many bits so unexpected
Colours seem to be so similar in shade and shape
difficult to imagine the length of time this will take
Suddenly gaining a reprieve from grass bits or sky
as you put in that crucial bit of a head, a vase or an eye
Gathering momentum now as the task is nearing the end
hoping there is nothing missing as on this you now depend
Finally you stare in wonder at the incredible sight
of your completed work of art which has taken you all night!

Tracey Monaghan

The Man Who Thrived On Risks

He played Russian Roulette when the craving for risk became too strong. All his life he had lived on the edge. He liked it like that. Everyday 'stuff' bored him to depression.

Buying food, buying clothes, paying the gas bill, checking the bank statement, it was grinding him to dust.

"Soul destroying," he would have said if he admitted to having a soul.

Now he was retired and safe, he had to drag himself out of bed in the morning. The day stretched like a long track through petty, mind-numbing banality.

He had never had a lasting relationship. Everyone bored him eventually. He saw other men his age, happily retired, engrossed in a multitude of activities. Family trees, gardening, golf, and, God almighty, cruises.

His loathing for such occupations was absolute. He likened these men to stuffed pillows with heads filled with putty. He thought them barely alive. And again, he spun the chamber and put the revolver barrel into his right ear.

At the click, he sighed. So many times, he had played this game and even here a certain lassitude crept upon him. Would even this game of chance pall?

What could he do? He would have to give in and abandon his risky play.

Slowly he fitted six bullets into their chambers.

Regretfully he closed the gun and placed the end of the barrel once more into his ear.

No risk now. This was a certainty.

Maureen C Bell

The Nosey Neighbour

Right – everybody's out of the house now, time to get on.
Think I'll clean the front windows and try to see what's going
on today – you miss so much working out the back!

There's James and his common-law wife - people say they've
done wonders with that house, but bright green for the front
bedroom, please! I need my sun-specs to look at it in daylight.
Their window-boxes are nice, but the number of times the
plants change - I know for a fact they're not grown from seed –
ready to plant, that's what they cheat with - anyone can grow
them! A seed's much more challenging – you wouldn't catch
me planting ready-made flowers!

Ah - there they go again, the two merry widows, probably off
to the Bingo. They're always together, not short of a bob or two
either, you often see them coming back from town with
Fenwick's and John Lewis Bags, I mean it's not as if you get
the bargains there that you get in the market is it? They must
have money to burn!

Looks like he's having problems next door with the cats again
– look at the state of his lawn, he'll be out there soon with his
bucket and trowel picking up their leavings – disgusting things,
mind you, I think the cats know he doesn't like them, strange
how they only seem to pick on his garden, I mean, we all hate
cats' mess, but don't advertise it to them by putting trays of tea
bags in the garden in silver trays so they'll be showing up in the
dark too, supposed to be a deterrent I think, wonder what he'll
use now! I hope he doesn't go back to the hose with fluorescent
stripes on again, it really lowers the tone - silly old so and so!

Get the flags out! She's actually opened the curtains today at
number ten.

Honestly, I really think there's some strange goings-on over there - different men coming out at all hours, back-packing every weekend, and her a psychology teacher, keeps funny hours if you ask me - never know who's going to appear next! Back yard's a disgrace too, so I hear, dirty old banger hogging the space, makes you wonder where she hangs her washing! Putting in new windows! She wants the council to do a clear up first, and as for her front garden, it comes to something when you've got to pay men to have your lawn cut, far cheaper to get a mower I would have thought!

Spotted him from number seven juggling on his front lawn last night - well have you ever? His wife seems sensible enough, mind you, I hear they haven't got a telly, no kids either - well what's left? I wouldn't be without 'Casualty' on a Saturday night, they don't know what they're missing!

Now him from number two, he's a real mystery, can't work him out at all, keeps himself to himself. Poor man though - you can't help feeling a bit sorry for him, his mam looked after him all those years, only to end up in a mental home. Often wonder where he goes with his video camera on a Saturday afternoon, looks like an 'anorak' to me, typical train spotter type. Keeps his garden nice though - works well over 9 o'clock some nights in it.

Three steps forward and two back, that's what that pair were doing last week from number twenty, in the middle of the day too - him a retired constable! Wonder if she works, not too often I think, judging by the number of times they roll home in that state! He goes on the waggon now and again; you don't see him for months sometimes. It's amazing to think of him doing voluntary work with the elderly - I hope it's during his 'dry' spells or the poor old dears will be passing out with the fumes!

I wonder who the people will be moving in that empty house three doors up there - I just hope they're not the sort who want to know everybody else's business, I can't stand people like that - I really can't!

There that's better - you can see more out of these windows now!

Tracey Monaghan

Printed in Poland
by Amazon Fulfillment
Poland Sp. z o.o., Wrocław

50477972R10085